Not Exactly Normal

Devin Brown

Eerdmans Books for Young Readers
Grand Rapids, Michigan • Cambridge, U.K.

To Sharon, who always encouraged me to write
—D.B.

Text © 2005 by Devin Brown
Published in 2005 by Eerdmans Books for Young Readers
An imprint of Wm. B. Eerdmans Publishing Company
255 Jefferson S.E., Grand Rapids, Michigan 49503
P.O. Box 163, Cambridge CB3 9PU U.K.
www.eerdmans.com/youngreaders

05 06 07 08 09 10   8 7 6 5 4 3 2 1

Library of Congress Cataloging-in-Publication Data
Brown, Devin.
Not exactly normal / written by Devin Brown.
p. cm.
Summary: A sixth-grader at St. Luke's Episcopal School sets out to have a mystical
experience and learns valuable lessons about himself and the world along the way.

ISBN 0-8028-5283-1 (alk. paper)

[1. Mysticism--Fiction. 2. Self-perception--Fiction. 3. Schools--Fiction.] I. Title.

PZ7.B81293No 2005
[Fic]--dc22
2004020443

Cover image photolibrary.com pty. ltd. / Image Stock
Book design by Matthew Van Zomeren

Contents

1.	Part of the Main?	1
2.	Not Exactly Normal	28
3.	Question Time	49
4.	An Ug and a Yuck	71
5.	Noodling	82
6.	The Extraordinary Ordinary	103
7.	Synchronicity	117
8.	Seeing a Pattern	141
9.	No Man Is an Island	161
10.	It's Been Real	190
11.	Middle C	210
	Read More About It	229

1

Part of the Main?

Mr. Phillips started morning reflections by taking his black dry-erase marker—the one he used when he wanted to write something beautifully—and putting four words in large calligraphy letters on the white marker board in front of the classroom:

Part of the Main

Turning to our class he said: "These words come from a famous sermon by John Donne that you're not supposed to study until you are seniors in high school. So six years from now, don't anyone tell

1

Mrs. Griswald you learned about it here."

Mrs. Griswald was the twelfth grade English teacher at St. Ann's, the Episcopal upper-school in Deerfield.

This was an example of Mr. Phillips' idea of a joke.

"John Donne wrote this famous sermon a long time ago, around four hundred years ago." Mr. Phillips paused to let this fact sink in. "He was the pastor at St. Paul's Cathedral in London, England. St. Paul's is a church in some ways like St. Luke's, but lots bigger and lots older. Pastor Donne was pretty old himself at the time, and one afternoon he was trying to write his Sunday sermon when all of a sudden he heard the church bell start ringing.

"Can anyone guess why the bell was ringing?"

———

I sat in the first seat of the second row in Mr. Phillips' sixth-grade class at St. Luke's Episcopal K-8.

This was not my assigned seat.

Unlike most of the other teachers at St. Luke's,

Mr. Phillips did not have assigned seats. Even without assigned seats, everyone always sat in the same place every day.

It's a fact: no one would ever think of sitting in someone else's spot. So really it was just the same as if we had assigned seats. Mr. Phillips was not exactly what I would call a normal sixth grade teacher, but then St. Luke's was not exactly what I would call a normal school.

———

". . . Alex Epstein, why do you think the bell John Donne heard was ringing?" Mr. Phillips sometimes called on people because they raised their hand, but most of the time he just called on someone. So it was a good idea to always be ready.

Alex Epstein, my best friend, sat in the third seat of the third row—not right next to me, but close enough. The only people who called him Alex were his parents and Mr. Phillips. To everyone else he was Nitro, as in nitroglycerine, because of his favorite hobby. Nitro liked making rockets—a lot. And his rockets had a tendency, well, to accidentally explode

3

before they and the little man he put inside each one made it back to earth.

"Was the bell ringing because it was time for church?" Nitro asked, a smile showing below his mop of curly brown hair.

———

It's a fact: when people described Nitro, they almost always called him good-natured. By this they meant that 1) he was the kind of person who never gave up, and 2) he did not focus on himself. We had been best friends for a long time, and as far as I could tell, nothing ever got him down. Nitro was about two inches shorter than I was and had a build you might call wiry—thin but strong. His being wiry and good-natured made him good in sports.

Really good.

Nitro's family was Jewish, the kind that celebrated the Jewish holidays but also had a Christmas tree and a plastic Santa on their roof that looked like he was halfway in and halfway out of the chimney. You could say this made Nitro somewhat not exactly normal. When he was a first grader, he had gone to

4

Winston Elementary. In second grade he switched to St. Luke's. Once when I asked him why he transferred, he said, "It's a lot easier to be Jewish in a school with some religion, than in one with no religion."

And that was all he ever said about it.

———

"That, Alex, is a good answer because back then they did ring the bell when it was time for church to start, just as many churches still do today. But that's not the reason they were ringing the bell John Donne heard.

"Does anyone else have an idea?"

———

St. Luke's Episcopal—which, you could say, was quite traditional in a lot of ways—was, first of all, small, really small. There was just one of every class from kindergarten up to eighth grade. On top of this, there were only twenty students in each class. Twenty kindergarteners, twenty first graders, twenty second graders, twenty every grade. A total of 180 students in the whole school.

St. Luke's was small, and it wanted to stay that way. For one reason, the school had to fit into the education annex of St. Luke's Episcopal Church, a church that was not small, but not exactly big. Even if it had more classrooms or bigger classrooms, St. Luke's the school would not want to be bigger. The headmaster liked to point out that the public school in Winston was big, and that St. Luke's, which was the only other school in town, gave students a choice.

By this he really meant it gave their parents a choice.

My parents had been choosing to send me to St. Luke's since kindergarten, but I didn't mind. After all those years with most of the same classmates, I felt like I belonged, at least most of the time.

You could say that I liked our town too. Winston, Massachusetts was small, like St. Luke's, and was located in the western side of the state. The closest real city—one with a Wal-Mart and a McDonald's—was Deerfield, ten miles away.

Curtis Winston Elementary, on the south side of town, was free. St. Luke's, located near the center of

Winston on the square, cost. Not a lot, but some. St. Luke's the church helped pay for part. That way, the headmaster said, St. Luke's would not be elitist.

Winston Elementary had a fleet of shiny yellow buses, and that's how most of its students got to school. St. Luke's did not have buses. It had kids who walked, kids who rode bikes, and kids who carpooled. Winston Elementary had a big, fancy gym with pull-out bleachers. St. Luke's used the parking lot for P. E. classes, except when it was raining. Then we used the all-purpose room, except when it was a lunch period.

Winston Elementary had recently acquired technology. This meant that they had computers in every classroom. St. Luke's had recently acquired white dry erase boards in every classroom.

Winston Elementary had students who were Episcopalian, Catholic, Quaker, Baptist, Presbyterian, Jewish, Lutheran, Methodist, other religions, and no religion. There was no weekly chapel and definitely no school prayer. St. Luke's also had students who were Episcopalian, Catholic, Quaker, Baptist, Presbyterian, Jewish, Lutheran, Methodist, other religions, and no religion. But St. Luke's had chapel every Wednesday and prayers at certain big stuff like graduation, the annual Christmas concert, and fund-raisers.

At St. Luke's, Mr. Phillips liked to say, you could wear anything you wanted as long as it was a pair of khaki or navy pants and a shirt with a collar and no writing. If you were a girl, if you wanted, you could wear a khaki or navy skirt instead of khaki or navy pants. At Winston Elementary you could wear what-ever you wanted.

So were students at St. Luke's any different from students at Curtis Winston?

I had friends from church and friends from swim-ming lessons who went to the public school. It's a fact: they didn't seem any more different from St. Luke's students than St. Luke's students seemed dif-ferent from each other.

Winston Elementary mostly had teachers who went to college only so they could be school teachers, not because they really wanted to read and study more. St. Luke's had some of that kind of teachers, too.

It also had Mr. Phillips. And as I mentioned, he

was, well, not exactly normal.

———

". . . Leda Johnson, how about you?" Mr. Phillips crossed to the far side of the classroom. "Why do you think they were ringing the church bell that John Donne heard?"

Leda sat on the other side of the classroom from me, in the fourth row, third seat. I know it's not really nice to say it, but Leda Johnson went far beyond not exactly normal.

Leda Johnson was, well, bizarre.

She was an only child, and she and her parents had moved to Winston from California when she was in third grade, to get away from what she called the sprawl. She had gone to Winston Elementary for one year and then transferred to St. Luke's at the start of fourth grade. She did not have any best friends in class—at least none that I knew of. She was not a bad person or mean, and everyone agreed she was the smartest in our class, maybe in the whole school.

Because of the way she talked, she sometimes seemed older than she was. Also it sometimes made you wish you had a Leda Dictionary.

It's a fact: Leda and I were almost exactly the same age. Her birthday was two days before mine. I knew this because 1) every Wednesday in chapel they announced the birthdays for that week, and 2) in a school as small as ours, you just know these things.

As it turned out, Leda and I were the only ones in the class to have our birthdays in December. This meant that we had started school later than everyone else. You might say that made us both a little not exactly normal in the same way, if that makes any sense.

Her blond hair was long and straight—like the rest of her. And maybe because of some special California hair spray she used, it always seemed to shine.

It's a fact: when the light hit her golden hair and her wire-rimmed glasses just right, they gave off, well, a nice sort of shimmer.

But she was still bizarre.

As I mentioned, St. Luke's was pretty strict about what you could and could not wear to school—except for your feet. In the shoe department it was pretty much anything goes, although most students just wore sneakers.

That day Leda was wearing a pair of leather boots that she called her Go-Goes. They were glossy white and had zippers instead of laces. They came up about halfway to her knees. I thought they made her look like a Power Ranger or something.

And Leda's footwear was just the tip of her bizarreness iceberg.

"Was the bell ringing to tell what the correct time was, the way churches in the foremost cities have a bell that automatically rings on the hour and every fifteen minutes thereafter? Well, not really a bell but a computerized digital recording of a bell?" Leda asked.

"No, but that, Leda, is also a very good answer because the church bells at St. Paul's in London and at a lot of other big churches do ring to tell the time, and that was important four hundred years ago when no one, not even rich people, had wrist watches."

———

Mr. Phillips was, first of all, young, really young for a teacher. He was definitely a lot younger than the normal teacher at either Winston Elementary or St. Luke's. We knew exactly how young because Mr. Phillips had told us on the first day of school that he had just turned twenty-four.

Second, Mr. Phillips was married to Pastor Jill, the assistant rector of St. Luke's the church. Mr. Phillips told our class that he had met Pastor Jill back when she was just Jill. This was another example of his idea of a joke. It meant that they met before she became a pastor, when they were studying together at the seminary. Mr. Phillips also told us that they had been married for two years and what date their anniversary was. He told us a lot of things that had nothing to do with school. Things you would never need to know for a test.

And this was the biggest way that Mr. Phillips was not exactly a normal teacher.

There were other ways that Mr. Phillips was not exactly normal for a sixth-grade teacher. One was that he didn't always teach English first period, math second period, social studies third period, and so on.

One day he might teach social studies first; the next day we might have science first. One day he might teach math for two periods and not any English. Or he might teach English twice, once in the morning and again after lunch.

Mixing up the schedule was supposed to help us pay attention.

At St. Luke's there were several groups of teachers. There were teachers that students liked, and then there were teachers the Parents' Board liked. There were the teachers that the students didn't like, and then there were the teachers that, according to certain rumors, the Parents' Board, well, had concerns about.

Mr. Phillips was one of the few teachers that both the Parents' Board and the students liked. Really liked.

I was glad that St. Luke's and Mr. Phillips were not exactly what I would call normal. Recently I had begun wondering how normal or not normal I was myself. And sometimes I found myself wishing that I were a little less ordinary.

I was average in sports—better than average in

swimming, but worse than average in soccer, which was not great because soccer was sort of *the* big thing in Winston. I was average in music — good enough to sing in St. Luke's Concert Choir but not good enough to be in Twenty-and-One, the school's best musical group, made up of six sixth graders, seven seventh graders, and eight eighth graders who played shiny brass handbells. I could play the piano, but not in the in-front-of-people way.

I was slightly above average in being funny, very slightly above average. If anyone ever thought that I was really above average funny, all they needed to do was to hang around Nitro for about two minutes. He was funny.

I was average in height for a sixth grader and average in weight. I had average length hair that was an average color, right between brown and blonde. You could say I was above average in intelligence and I was a pretty good writer. But our class had lots of students who were smart.

Really smart.

———

". . . Todd Farrel, how about you?" Mr. Phillips came back over to my side of the classroom. "Can you think of a reason that the church bell was ringing?"

Nitro had taken my first answer—to say church was starting. Leda had taken my second answer—to tell the time. But I was ready with a third answer.

Like I mentioned, it was a good idea to always be ready in Mr. Phillips' class.

"Were they ringing the bell because there was a fire?" I asked.

"No, but that, Todd, is also a very good answer because four hundred years ago they did ring the church bells when there was a fire. These different reasons—to call people to church, to tell the time, and to announce a fire—all had different rings and sometimes even different bells that people could understand. A bell says to us, 'Pay attention—something special is happening.'

"On that afternoon when he was trying to write his sermon, John Donne heard a special ring of a special bell. He heard the bell they rang when someone was dying." Mr. Phillips paused a few seconds to let

15

this fact sink in.

"When John Donne heard the death bell ringing, he wondered: Who is this person who is dying? What if this person dying is someone really important? What if this person is someone I know?" Mr. Phillips looked around the room, and it got a little spooky for a second.

"And then all at once, John Donne got an idea for his sermon. He said that the bell was ringing to remind him it did not matter if this person was an important person in the community. It did not matter if he knew this person or not. He said the bell reminded him that no man — or woman — is an island because each person is connected to the mainland of humanity. Each person is 'part of the main.'"

As Mr. Phillips said this last part, he tapped each word on the board with his marker to get us to all sit up and really listen.

"'No man is an island.' Do you believe that?" Mr. Phillips paused and looked around the room.

"Each one is a 'part of the main.' Is that true?" He paused again.

I wondered if Mr. Phillips was going to start calling on people, but then I realized that these were what Mr. Phillips called rhetorical questions, questions just to think about. Then Mr. Phillips underlined the words and added a big calligraphy question mark so that now it read:

Part of the Main?

And that was the end of morning reflections.

From where I sat in the first seat of the second row, I had a good view of the collection of stuff push-pinned to the bulletin board behind Mr. Phillips' desk. There was a picture of Mr. Phillips and Pastor Jill on skis. Mr. Phillips' wavy black hair had been really long then, and it flowed out from under his stocking cap. He was pretty tall, and in the picture Pastor Jill only came up to his shoulders. Next to the picture was an extra big push pin that held a thick stack of memos from the headmaster.

It's a fact: Mr. Phillips never seemed to do anything with the headmaster's memos. He just kept

17

sticking them up with his extra big push pin.

Next to the big stack of memos was a poem in hand-written calligraphy letters with a picture drawn underneath. From my seat, I could barely just read it. And when I wasn't paying attention, something that happened more often than you might think, I looked at it a lot. One day as the class was going to lunch, I had stayed behind and asked Mr. Phillips about it. He had explained that the passage came from an old book called *The Canterbury Tales*.

In the opening Prologue, all the characters were described. The lines by Mr. Phillips' desk were about someone named the Oxford Cleric, an old word which meant scholar. The passage read:

An Oxford Cleric, still a student though,
had studied logic long ago.
His horse was thinner than a rake, and
he was not fat, I undertake.

He had a lanky look and a thoughtful
stare; the thread that made his coat
was bare.

He preferred having twenty volumes
        of philosophy, than costly clothes,
        food, or finery.

Whatever money from his friends he
        took, he spent on lessons or
        another book!

Honest goodness filled his speech.
        Gladly would he learn, and
        gladly teach.

In the picture under the words there was a skinny young man sitting at a big desk. He had a smile on his face and piles of books all around him. When I had asked who had drawn the picture and done the lettering, Mr. Phillips said that he had done it himself— another way he was not exactly a normal teacher.

I sometimes wondered if maybe Mr. Phillips had put the passage up by his desk because he wanted to be like the character it described. I liked the last line best: *Gladly would he learn, and gladly teach.* That fit Mr. Phillips.

Through the classroom window that was even with my desk, I could see the car that Mr. Phillips and Pastor Jill drove. It was in the same place it sat every day: the last spot in the parking lot, under the big oak tree, next to the old church cemetery. That day the car was covered in a blanket of snow except for a tiny opening that had been scraped from the front windshield. When the wind blew, the powdery snow swirled around the car like a little tornado.

Winter came early in western Massachusetts. And December in Winston could be cold, really cold. Mr. Phillips' car reminded me of the Oxford Cleric's horse because it was small and, well, it's a fact: it was old. The clothes that Mr. Phillips wore were not thin or worn out like the Oxford Cleric's, but he never wore a tie—another way he was not exactly a normal St. Luke's teacher—just a shirt with a collar and no writing and khaki or navy pants. Maybe because he was a teacher now, his hair was shorter than in the picture of him and Pastor Jill.

One way that Mr. Phillips was like the other teachers at St. Luke's was that he started out each day with morning reflections during homeroom.

Some days Mr. Phillips read a Bible verse, but just as often he would read words from a song, or a poem, or who knows what.

All during school that day I thought about those words: *No man is an island. Each one is a part of the main.*

Leda hung out by herself a lot at school. Did this mean she was an island?

I had a best friend in class, some good friends, and some just regular friends. I knew almost all the kids at St. Luke's. Without getting all gushy, you could also say that I had parents that I knew loved me and a younger brother in third grade who was pretty cool, for a younger brother.

Did these things make me a part of the main?

On the other hand, sometimes I liked being alone to think about things. Was this being an island? And if it was—was being an island always bad?

———

Mr. Phillips ended school that day with social studies, and at the very end of class he gave us all another thing to think about.

21

"All right, class. Before you go home today, I want to make an announcement. You all know that in the sixth grade at St. Luke's, we end Winter Term with a big social studies report."

The whole class groaned.

"Please hold your applause," Mr. Phillips continued. "We have twelve days left until Christmas vacation. Our last day of school will be a Monday, and don't anyone ask why we have to go to school on that Monday when Winston Elementary starts Christmas break on Friday. Just remember: St. Luke's is not exactly a normal school.

"I am passing out the instruction sheet for your report. On the last day before Christmas break, we will cancel all afternoon classes, and each person will read his or her social studies project aloud in front of the class and then hand it in. Your report will count for one-fourth of your social studies grade."

The bell rang just as Mr. Phillips said "grade."

He always knew just when the final bell was going to ring.

"That special bell is ringing not to remind you that no man or woman is an island, but to get you started thinking about what your topic is going to be. To-morrow during social studies, each of you will have to tell the class what you are thinking about writing on for your report. Are there any questions?"

Mr. Phillips paused a moment to see if there were. Then he finished by saying, "Well, it's been real."

Mr. Phillips always said "Well, it's been real" at the end of each day, a phrase he said came from the 1960s. This was his not-exactly-normal way to say everyone could go.

———

As I walked the eleven blocks home, my boots left the faintest of footprints in the snow-packed sidewalk. When I turned and looked behind me, I could just barely see where I had passed. I had on my warmest coat, my stocking hat and scarf, and my thick gloves. My backpack with my homework bounced on my shoulders as I walked.

It was only four-thirty, but the slanting, Decem-ber sun—which had already been low in the sky when school let out—had disappeared during choir practice for the Christmas concert. A cold bite had come into the air. The streetlights were coming on and sparkled off the snow crystals that clung to the trees and bushes.

It was two-and-a-half weeks until Christmas, and almost every other house I passed had put decorations up. Winston had two kinds of decorators. The Early Birds put up everything on the day after Thanksgiving. Then they took all it down and had their tree on the curb and the carpet vacuumed before lunchtime on December 26th.

The second kind, the Decorations Police, thought, and sometimes even complained, that Christmas decorations should not go up until closer to Christmas.

As I looked over to the town square, I could see the lights from the little white candles that the town of Winston always put up in the windows of fire station, the library, and city hall from the first of December until the end of January. Decorations which could be said to celebrate lots of different holidays, or no holiday, just winter.

My family was one of those who didn't have really strong feelings either way, but we almost always waited until the day before Christmas to put up our tree and then left it up until Epiphany, twelve days after Christmas. In the month leading up to Christmas Eve, we put out our Advent wreath with its four candles, one to light each week. We also hung up our Advent calendar with its little windows to open each day.

As I walked home, I was glad that at least some families put their decorations up early. They gave off a friendliness that was needed now with the days so short.

Without the decorations, the winter darkness was, well, just dark.

As I looked down the block, the Christmas lights on the houses seemed like reflections of the first stars in the deep purple sky. From one of the stores back on the square, I could hear notes from a Christmas song too faint to recognize. The lights, the stars, and the far off music gave me a kind of a mysterious feeling inside that I couldn't quite describe, but I liked.

Sort of a tingle, but deeper.

We lived a little over a mile from St. Luke's, far enough for me to take the Eastside carpool if I wanted. My brother, Davis, always rode with his friend Ned whose mother worked in the St. Luke's office, but I liked to walk. And usually I walked by myself. Some sixth graders would complain that a mile was too long to walk. It's a fact: some would complain about having to walk from their house to the corner carpool stop and, no kidding, would try to get their parents to drive them.

In the morning, walking helped me wake up and get ready. I suppose Leda might say that walking home gave me time "to process my day" or something. I would just say that my long walk gave me the chance to think over everything that had happened. By the time everyone was ready to leave and the Eastside carpool had made all its stops, I would be nearly home anyway.

I had a little homework to do that night, but nothing major. As I walked, I wondered what my mother was making for supper. You could say she was the fun kind of mother, who liked to joke with me and my brother and was not totally corny. At the same time she was also the firm kind of mother, the kind who said she wanted her family to have a "proper" dinner each night and really meant it—a whole-family-sit-down-together dinner with good nutrition, correct table manners, and even a blessing where we all held hands.

When she would talk with Davis or me about something that we shouldn't be doing, something that happened more often than you might think, she liked us to come to what she called a "consensus." This was her fun but firm way to say stop doing it.

My mom and dad were also big on family conversation around the dinner table. Really big. So I also wondered what they would say when I told them about what had happened that day at school—not what Mr. Phillips had said at morning reflections, and not what Mr. Phillips had announced at the end of social studies.

I wondered what my parents would say when I told them about what had happened during lunch period with Leda Johnson.

2

Not Exactly Normal

"Our prayer tonight was written by John Cennick, an Anglican priest who was born in 1718 and died in 1755," my father said as he opened the big book called *One Hundred Mealtime Blessings*. "Anglican, in case anyone wants to know, means 'belonging to the Church of England.'"

As we sat around the table, I took my mother's hand, who took my brother's hand, who took my father's hand, who took my other hand.

Be present at our table, Lord.
Be here and everywhere adored.

Thy creatures bless, and grant that we
May feast in Paradise with Thee.

"Amen," said my father.

"Amen," my mother, my brother Davis, and I said.

"Today during lunch, you know what Leda Johnson told about?" I asked.

"Davis, would you please pass your father the mashed potatoes?"

"No, what did Leda tell about?" my father wanted to know.

"She told about a mystical experience that she had."

"A misses what?" asked Davis as he swallowed a big forkful of potatoes.

"Davis, when you talk with your mouth full, we can't understand you. And I thought we had reached a consensus about taking off your baseball cap when we're at the table. You know—to show proper respect for our proper supper."

My mother said this in a way that showed she was laughing at herself a little. "And besides, we all want to see your beautiful head of hair, especially your father. It reminds him of something from long ago."

"It's true, son," said my father, who was not exactly bald but who definitely had more head than hair. "Oh, too true."

"Sorry, Mom, I forgot." Davis took off his cap and when no one was looking put it on the head of our Irish setter, Cathode, who sat under the table next to Davis's chair during meals.

Davis looked enough like me for most people to think we were brothers. Our hair was about the same color and the same length. But he was small for his age and was the only one in our family who wore glasses. He had just gotten a new pair that were round and black, and they made him look, well, what Leda might have called "pensive."

"A mystical experience," I answered.

"I think she might be a little young to start having mystical experiences. Davis, take some cauliflower," my mother said, passing him the bowl. "Don't you think so, James?"

"Don't I think what?" asked my father, using his fork to make a crater in the middle of his mashed potatoes.

"Davis, you need to take more than one piece. It's full of micronutrients," said my mother.

"I hate cauliflower," said Davis, looking at the bowl of steaming, white vegetables.

"Yes, I know you do. Take some anyway. Look at your father. He's eating cauliflower, and, I must say, serving as a wonderful role model for the young boys of the world at this moment."

My father made the sound of an airplane in a banked turn, opened his mouth wide, and took a big bite. "Steamed cauliflower—my favorite. And you know," he said, raising his eyebrows up and down, "I've heard that it's quite good for you."

My father sometimes kidded about my mother's enthusiasm—obsession, you could say—for proper nutrition, but he supported it. He even cooked once or twice a week—usually breakfast—and it was pretty good. When he didn't cook, he always helped to clean up.

My mother put a small portion of cauliflower on Davis's plate. In our family this was called a "no thank you" portion. No matter what it was called, you still had to eat it.

She pointed the spoon at Davis in a way that said something. Then she turned back to my father. "Don't you think she's a little young to start having mystical experiences?"

"Well, how old is she? Gravy, please."

"James, the Johnsons have lived across the street since they moved here. Leda's always been in the same grade as Todd. How old do you think she is?"

"Ummm, let's see . . ." My dad pretended like he didn't know our ages and wrinkled his forehead as he chewed.

"We both just turned twelve, Dad," I whispered to him behind my hand.

"Ah, yes, thanks, son," whispered my father. "Twelve," he said turning to my mother.

"Honestly, James, sometimes I swear you're no better than the boys."

"Milk, please," I said, jumping in when I saw the chance.

"I totally agree with you," my dad said. "Would you please pass the *skinless*, *boneless*, *grilled* chicken back this way?"

"You agree that Leda is too young?"

"No, that I'm no better than the boys. Thank you, Davis."

"Oh, James, now be serious. Tell us what you think."

"About Leda? Well, I suppose it depends on what kind of mystical experience she had."

"Are there different kinds?" Davis asked as he slipped Cathode a piece of cauliflower under the table.

"Sure," said my father, hunting through the plate of chicken for a piece of white meat. "Big ones, little ones, grouchy ones . . ." Davis and I laughed.

"James, stop," said my mother. "Davis, do not listen to him. He is being very silly tonight. And take some beets."

"I hate beets," said Davis.

"Your father is having beets. They're full of micronutrients."

"Oh no, not *beets*!" My father made a face like they were full of radioactivity.

"See, Mom," said Davis. "Dad won't eat them either."

"James, you're not helping the situation." As

she said this, my mother put an extra big spoonful of beets on my dad's plate.

"Wow, Emma, that is an extremely generous 'no thank you' portion."

"And I don't want any either," said Davis.

"You eat some cauliflower. Now," my mother said in a tone that was not exactly her consensus voice. Turning back to my father, she said, "You should at least try them, James."

"I know I should, but, well, beets and cauliflower in the same meal? You know, a man can only do so much. Where's Cathode?"

"Under the table, Dad," I said.

"Here, boy. You want some nice beets?" said my father, pretending like he was going to give Cathode a piece of a beet.

My mother gave my father the look, half pretending, but half really meaning it.

"Ah, smart dog," said my father as Cathode appeared uninterested. It seems that a dog can only do so much too. Cute hat there, fella. Well, it looks like I will have to eat these beets. You know, boys, I've heard that they're really good for you."

"What's a mystical experience, Mom?" asked Davis.

"Well, you could say a mystical experience is when a person experiences something strange or out of the ordinary, something that he or she can't explain."

"Like what?" Davis persisted.

My mother paused a moment to think. "Well, if you knew something was going to happen before it did happen, or if you did something that seemed impossible, that would be a mystical experience. Sometimes when several unlikely coincidences happen at the same time, people might call that a mystical experience."

"A famous psychiatrist named Carl Jung had a special name for the unexplained occurrence of unconnected events to produce a specific result," said my father. "He called it *synchronicity*."

"Some people who have had a mystical experience tell about a vision they had," my mother continued. "They might see God, or an angel. They might suddenly understand something they never understood before. They might see a person far away, or even dead people sometimes."

"Dead people!" Davis opened his eyes wide. "Uh, I don't think I want to be having any mystical experiences."

"*Synchronicity* comes from two Greek words which mean 'happening at the same time,'" my father added.

"Leda said that she saw a long, dark tunnel," I explained. "At the end of the tunnel was a bright light. She said that she heard a voice that told her she had been three other people besides Leda. She said that the voice told her she was going to go back in time and find her three other lives."

"She might be referring to something like reincarnation," said my father. "It's a belief that Hindus, Buddhists, and some other religious groups have."

"Mom, do I have to finish all this cauliflower?" Davis pointed at the slightly-dented pile on his plate.

"Plato believed in reincarnation," my dad continued.

"I suppose you've had enough."

"Good. What did Leda say happened then, after

she saw the light and heard the voice?" Davis asked.

"Then she said her mystical experience ended," I said. "But she said just before the voice went away, it told her that tomorrow she would start going back to her other three lives."

"That sounds creepy," said Davis.

"I think it's kind of interesting." I looked over at my mother. "Do you think it could be true?"

"Do I think it could be true? Well, you've asked a complicated question, Todd. Let me ask you a question. Would you say that Leda always tells the exact truth about everything else?"

"I would say that usually she does, but sometimes I guess maybe she doesn't. I don't really know her that well."

"Then maybe we shouldn't be too quick to judge." My mother paused and looked like she was thinking something over. "Even though the Johnsons have been here for a few years, I wonder if maybe Leda is still feeling a little, well, unconnected. Like she's still the new girl in town or something. Who knows? Maybe she would just like to be noticed a little. Sometimes we just don't know what someone else is going through."

"More green tea, Emma?" My father held up the teapot.

"Not just yet, James, thank you. Maybe we should invite Leda to come over with her parents the next time we host the Occasional Saturday Night Healthy Supper Club. The Epsteins could bring Nitro, too."

"Dad, may I be excused?" Davis wanted to know.

"After you finish your skim milk. What about homework for tonight?"

"I've got to make up five more Superheroes for my art project." Davis put down his empty glass. "But it's not due until next week. Here, Cathode."

Davis retrieved his baseball cap, took his dirty dishes into the kitchen, and headed upstairs. "Good supper, Mom. Sorry about the beets, but a boy can only do so much, you know. Come on, fella."

"And what about you, Todd?" my father asked.

"I have to do five square roots, read a story from our unit on heroes, and come up with a topic for my social studies report." I headed into the kitchen with my dishes.

"Homework before TV," my dad called after me. This was something he said every night. "What are we watching this evening?"

"A movie called *Sorry, Wrong Monster*. It comes on at seven-thirty," I said, starting up the steps to join Davis in our room.

"I'll have that tea now, James, if there's some left," my mother said.

"My pleasure, Emma."

As I went up the stairs, I heard my father say something about bizarre California ideas as he started to clear the rest of the table, and my mother going on about the importance of creative imagination for young people today.

———

Up in our room I read the assigned story from our unit on heroes and finished my five square-root problems. During math that day Mr. Phillips had said, "You're not supposed to learn how to figure square roots until two years from now. So don't anyone tell Mrs. Allbright that I taught you how to do them." Mrs. Allbright was the eighth grade teacher at St. Luke's.

Nitro had asked, "Why do we have to learn to do square roots by hand when we can do them faster on the calculator? They don't do them by hand at Curtis Winston."

Mr. Phillips had said, "Just keep telling yourself: St. Luke's is not exactly a normal school."

I took out a clean sheet of paper from my desk drawer and stared at its blank whiteness.

I was a pretty good writer, but what I wrote about was always so ordinary. I wanted to come up with a report topic that was not so normal, one that would be different from the others, something different from what I usually did.

I stared at the paper and thought and chewed on my pencil and scratched my head and stared at the paper some more. Then I did what I always did when I got stuck—I put down my pencil and I rubbed my eyebrows.

It's a fact: rubbing your eyebrows usually will help you think better.

This time it didn't help much. I thought some more and rubbed my eyebrows some more. Now you might be wondering why choosing a topic for my social studies report was such a big ordeal for me. I can tell you in one word.

Luxembourg.

———

Fourth grade at St. Luke's ends the year with everyone giving a report on a foreign country they've chosen.

I chose Luxembourg.

In some ways Luxembourg made sense. In case you don't know, Luxembourg is small, really small. And in one way that was good because I did not have to go searching through tons of books to find the important information.

It's a fact: in a country as small as Luxembourg, everything is important.

The written part of my report was fine. The problem came with trying to come up with stuff to put on the display table that each of us had in the all-purpose room for what was called the Parade of Nations. Each year, after all the reports are finished, everyone walks around with their parents, looks at things from the countries we have just heard about, and eats. Putting out special food from your country is a big part of it.

Nitro had picked France. For his display table he had put our little pieces of French bread and French cheese to snack on. He also had a bottle of French wine—unopened—and some French music playing from a CD. He had the flag of France draped over his table and a big display featuring famous French soccer players.

David Minstro had picked Scotland. On his table he had a real kilt and, no kidding, real Scottish bagpipes that people going by got to try to play. In case you don't know, bagpipes are not exactly the easiest instrument in the world to play. Most people when they blew into them made something between a loud squeak and a squawk. David had a big basket of Scottish shortbread to eat. Scottish shortbread tastes sort of like vanilla cookies, but smoother. I know because when no one was at my table I went over and ate about half of them. On a little TV David played a scene from the video of *Braveheart* where the Scots were fighting the British long ago.

You get the idea.

On my Luxembourg table I had a little picture of the Luxembourg flag that I found on the Internet because, well, where would you get a real one? I also had pictures of some stuff made in Luxembourg, pictures that I found on the Internet because of the same problem. And I had a bowl of potato chips to eat.

Next to the bowl I put a card that read, "It's a fact: people in Luxembourg consume slightly more potato chips per person than any other nationality in Europe."

In fifth grade there had been a math contest instead of a final project, so Luxembourg had been my last big report up until now. And you could say that for me it had been something of a disaster. This time I needed a topic that was good.

Really good.

By the way, it was during my Luxembourg project that I finally noticed Leda.

Before then I knew who she was, of course, but that was about it. She had chosen a country between India and Australia that no one had ever heard of called Kampuchea. This meant that at the Parade of Nations her table was next to mine alphabetically.

She set out this weird-smelling food that, well, made beets and cauliflower seem like a cheeseburger and fries. Every time someone stopped by her display, Leda did this strange little dance, played these tiny cymbals that went on her fingers, and then tried to get them to taste some of the weird food.

And that was when I started using the word bizarre to describe her.

———

After a few more minutes of thinking, I picked my pencil back up and wrote down one idea for my social studies report. Not a big idea, or even a medium one, more of an idea*ette*. I thought a little more and wrote down a second idea. Then finally a third. None of them sounded all that special, but they were the best I could come up with. I had written:

Ways We Celebrate Christmas Today
The Imports and Exports of My Hometown
The Highest Spots in the County

I decided it was definitely time to take a break.

"How's your Superhero project coming?" I asked Davis, who had crayons and drawing paper spread out over his desk.

"Mrs. Whitmore said I need to make up seven. I'm almost done with number three."

"Show me what you have so far."

Davis pushed his glasses back up on his nose and took two drawings out of his folder.

"This first one is Komodo Dragon Boy. He scratches criminals with his long claws and knocks them down with his heavy tail.

"This," Davis handed me his second picture, "is Asbestos the Human Torch. He has a belt that can spray out lit matches, a flaming torch, fire bombs, or a fire extinguisher, depending on which button he presses."

"Who's this guy with nothing but a cape on?"

Davis showed me the picture he had just finished. "That's Naked Man. He puts oil all over his skin so no one can hold on to him"

"Those are pretty good." I would never say it, except maybe to Nitro, but I thought my brother Davis was not exactly normal in the good way, like St. Luke's and Mr. Phillips.

Davis looked over his drawings. "I think so."

For the next fifteen minutes I tried to think of a more special topic for my report but had no luck. I had just decided to take another break when my father called us to come down for the movie.

You may find this hard to believe, but there are people who tell me they think my first name is interesting in the not-exactly-normal sense. Not a lot, but a few, well, maybe one or two people have told me this. And then they always want to know where "Todd" comes from—like did I have a grandfather or an uncle named Todd, or did my name come from another language or something.

It's a fact: there was no one in my family named Todd before me. No close friends of the family, no favorite character in my mother's favorite novel. Todd was not the name of the person who introduced my parents or the waiter on their first date. The real answer to why I was named Todd isn't very interesting. My dad's first name is James, Jim for short, and when I was born my parents wanted to give me a name that was a little less ordinary. So they named me Todd.

That was back when the name Todd was, well, kind of unusual.

In the twelve years since I was born there have been lots of parents who have wanted to name their children something a little less ordinary than Jim. This means that today my name isn't unusual, but it's not exactly normal, and that's okay with me. I mean, I'm glad that I'm not Jim or Bob, but I wouldn't want to have one of those first names that you can't tell if it's a boy or a girl, or if it's their first name or last. One of those names that the person always has to repeat over and over and then finally spell.

Something like Jarel or Devonte.

Now if that's your name, or your name is Jim, I'm not saying anything is wrong with that. It's just not me.

———

Sorry, Wrong Monster failed to give me any better ideas for a topic for my social studies report. Later as I was getting ready for bed, I decided I would have to go with The Imports and Exports of My Hometown—at least as my backup. As I lay in bed, I thought about everything that had happened that day at school.

It was dark in the room, but a faint light came in through the windows. I looked over at Davis. As usual, he was already fast asleep.

Like I usually did before falling asleep, I looked out the window next to my bed.

Down below, the street was empty, and the street-lights cast a soft glow on the snow-covered sidewalk. The wind had blown the night sky clear, and the winter stars twinkled in the vast openness. High above I could hear the eerie rush of the wind. Suddenly I was filled with a feeling that I couldn't name.

Sort of an ache for something, but for what I didn't know. It felt like a shiver, but one that Leda might have said was "solemn."

And all at once I came up with an idea.

"I know," I thought. "I'll do my report on mystical experiences. They are something not exactly normal. I'd like to find out more about them."

I fell asleep wondering what Leda Johnson was going to say the next day when she heard what my topic was.

3

Question Time

The next day at school, Leda Johnson was not exactly Leda Johnson.

She announced before homeroom that her name was now Katherine La Charmante. For the most part, Katherine La Charmante looked and acted a lot like Leda, except that instead of taking her red winter scarf off with her coat and hanging it up in the cloakroom, she wrapped it around her neck, let one end hang down, and threw the other end over her shoulder.

Also, when she remembered, instead of "the" and "this" she said "zee" and "zis."

I know that when you say someone's unique, you're not supposed to say they're very unique because unique already means one of a kind. This is the rule we were all taught. But Leda was definitely the exception. If anyone could be very unique, it was Leda.

Mr. Phillips looked around the room. "For morning reflections today, I wonder if anyone has a question he or she would like to ask?"

About once a week we had Question Time for morning reflections. As always, Mr. Phillips started Question Time by saying the same thing:

"Remember, a person who asks an honest question praises God."

I didn't know exactly what Mr. Phillips meant by this, but I liked it. Did it mean that it was good to question things? Or maybe that if we didn't know something we shouldn't pretend we did? Or was it something else?

David Minstro, who sat next to me, in the first row, first seat, raised his hand and asked what the twelve days of Christmas were and if this was the reason Mr. Phillips had assigned our reports twelve days before Christmas break. David was one of my good friends at school.

Mr. Phillips explained that a long time ago in England they celebrated Christmas for twelve days. Back then December 25th was just the first day of Christmas.

He said that in England now, they no longer celebrate the twelve days of Christmas. And despite the song that everyone gets sick of, nobody gives a partridge in a pear tree to their true love anymore — if they ever did.

He said that besides Christmas Day, the only other day they still celebrate in England is the day after Christmas, called Boxing Day. This is a day not for a boxing match but for remembering others who were less fortunate. He said that on December 26th the English give Christmas boxes to people who had helped them during the year — like their mailman or papergirl.

Mr. Phillips said that besides Christmas the only one of the twelve days that St. Luke's celebrates is Epiphany. Then he added, "As far as I know, the twelve days before Christmas break do not have any special name although I have heard that some teachers call them misery."

"That's a joke," Mr. Phillips said when no one got it. "Is there anyone else who has a question?"

Leda Johnson raised her hand.

"What is zis Epiphany?" asked Katherine La Charmante.

Mr. Phillips did not say anything about Leda's scarf or her way of saying this, which I thought was kind of interesting. He explained to us that Epiphany was the twelfth or last day of Christmas, the day the Wise Men had arrived to visit the Baby Jesus.

Leda raised her hand again.

"In the first book of a trilogy I was reading last night, the protagonist said that she had an epiphany. Is that the same thing?" she asked, forgetting to say zee instead of the.

Mr. Phillips explained that when Epiphany was capitalized it meant the special day when Jesus was shown to the Wise Men. Then Mr. Phillips grabbed the big, worn dictionary that sat on his desk and started looking up something—he did this a lot.

"But when epiphany is not capitalized," he continued as he turned the pages, "it means 'a sudden perception, a striking grasp of the truth because of a simple event, an illuminating discovery about someone or something,'" Mr. Phillips finished reading. Then he closed the dictionary and set it back down on the desk. "Does anyone else have a question?"

Theresa Anwar, who sat across the room from me—fourth row, first seat—raised her hand and asked what Mr. Phillips was going to get Pastor Jill for Christmas. Theresa was not one of my best friends or even one of my good friends—at least not yet. I would say she was a friend, but also that she was someone that I was, well, interested in.

Theresa had long dark hair and dark eyes that made her perfectly white teeth really stand out. You may think this is weird, but I swear that when she smiled, the room got a little brighter.

And if you think about it, that is something.

Theresa's family owned Anwar's, the Middle-Eastern restaurant in Winston. They had moved to America from Lebanon when Theresa was little and had moved to Massachusetts from New York this year just before school started.

———

Back in August on the first day of school, everyone was supposed to write for twenty minutes—no more, and no less—on something they had done over summer vacation. Mr. Phillips asked Theresa if she would mind writing on a special topic—on what it was like when she first came to America. He asked her to try to find a way to let the class "stand in her shoes."

Twenty minutes later, when everyone had to put down their pens and one at a time shared aloud what they had written, Theresa had read:

COMING TO AMERICA
by Theresa Anwar

When I first came to America, I was only six, so I cannot remember everything.

I remember there was a really long plane ride that I took with my mother. We had breakfast, and lunch, and supper on the plane and watched two movies. I filled every page of my notebook with pictures that I drew. Most of them were of my dad and my

*mom and me at the new apartment he had
written us about.*

I also slept a lot.

*And yes, I got a pair of wings from the
flight attendant, and at the time this was a
big deal.*

*When we got to New York, my father
was waiting on the other side of the
immigration tables to pick us up. And boy
was he happy! He kissed and hugged my
mom and me about a million times. My mom
and I were so happy that we kissed and
hugged him about a million times too. It had
been four months since we had seen him,
but he looked just the same.*

*Next he took us to the apartment that
he had rented for us. It was not far from the
restaurant he was the manager of, and it
was very nice. I really liked living several
stories up and looking out of my window at
birds flying down below and seeing what the
world must look like to them. We had many
good neighbors who came over to welcome*

us with all kinds of food that seemed strange
to me. Strange but delicious.

I only had one problem—English!
I couldn't understand what anyone was
saying! But this is not what made me really
mad. What was worse was that no one could
understand what I was saying! So one day I
decided to write on a piece of paper what I
wanted to tell them, and it looked like this.

Then Theresa had held up a sheet of paper with
Arabic writing on it.

Maybe trying to understand this can
help you to stand in my shoes.

Afterwards Mr. Phillips had taped up all the es-
says on the wall outside our classroom and left them
there for the next week so that everyone could look
at them. I read Theresa's a couple times and thought
about what it might mean to stand in someone else's
shoes.

56

Mr. Phillips said Theresa's question about what he was going to get Pastor Jill for Christmas was more complicated than we might think. He and Pastor Jill had agreed that they were not going to exchange presents this year—instead they were going to give each other a vacation trip. However, they were going to take this trip during spring break, because at Christmas they had to visit both of their families. And he said that, as we all would understand later, visiting family was not exactly a real vacation. So they were saving their money to go skiing in Vermont in March.

Mr. Phillips went on to say that he was also looking for either a book or a CD to give Pastor Jill on Christmas morning. And no, this was not breaking their agreement, because she was going to get him a book or a CD too. In answer to the class's puzzled looks, Mr. Phillips said this was another one of those things we would understand when we got older.

As I said, Theresa was someone that I was interested in. Now before you get the wrong idea, I should tell you a little something about my romantic history, or my lack thereof.

Right. During the winter of third grade I had my first official girlfriend. Her name was Mary Drummond, and she is still in the same class I am, although now we are just friends.

When I say just, I don't mean to suggest that we don't ever talk to each other now or that we feel weird when we're together or anything.

I am just saying that for about two weeks back in third grade, I was her boyfriend and she was my girlfriend, and everyone—including the rest of the class, our parents, and even Mrs. Whitmore, our teacher— knew it. And after it was over, we were and still are just like we were before. Friends. Which is a good thing, I think.

What exactly did it mean back in third grade that Mary Drummond and I were boyfriend and girlfriend?

I have no earthly idea.

Every so often now Mary and I will laugh about how we used to get in trouble for sending notes to each other during class when Mrs. Whitmore had her back turned or about how we told everyone we were going to get married.

We laugh now because we seemed so, well, so young then. And if that doesn't make you feel old, I guess nothing will.

So that was back in third grade, and there's not a lot more to tell to bring you up to the present.

In fourth grade I was Terri Donnelly's husband in a play that we did in class about the Pilgrims. I had to stand close to her a lot. Really close. And then I had to sort of hold her by her elbow and guide her into a fake log cabin made out of the cardboard box from a refrigerator.

Looking back, two things stand out.

1) I must admit that I kind of liked standing close to Terri Donnelly during all those days of play practice and then holding her by the elbow and guiding her around.

2) I am sure that no girl or woman, not even a Pilgrim girl or woman, ever liked being toted around like that.

After it was over, word got around that, well, let's

just say that word got around that Terri didn't enjoy being in the play as much as I did. I never knew if it was me personally or just the elbow thing, but when I heard that, it sort of ruined it, if you know what I mean.

Then last year in the fifth grade, I had what you might call my first and my only date, depending on how you define the word. I call it a date.

Every winter St. Luke's makes a little ice rink for skating over on the edge of the schoolyard. All this means is that after the ground freezes, but before the first snow, the school janitor gets out the old fire hose and lets the water run until it fills up this low area on the other side of the playground. The first week or so, the ice is really nice because they put a new, thin layer of water on it every night after everyone leaves. But after a couple snowfalls, it's not that great, and after a while they give it up altogether.

But at the beginning, like the start of winter itself, St. Luke's little ice rink is kind of a big deal. At least for fifth graders.

So after school on the second day that we could skate, I asked a girl from our class if she wanted to go skating that night after supper. Now before you start thinking that I was some sort of a Number One Lover Boy with all these cool lines, you need to know that asking a girl to go skating on the school ice rink was something that you do when you are in fifth grade, at least at St. Luke's.

Suave. That's the word I would like to say describes me deciding who I would ask to go skating. Or perhaps Mr. Suave. But what actually happened was we were just talking one day at lunch, and Nitro announced he was going to ask Sue Shuttleworth. Then David Minstro said he was going to ask Mary Drummond.

Now I don't know if I just didn't want to be the only one not asking someone, or if I was caught off guard by David saying he was going to ask my former fiancé, but when they looked at me and waited, I just sort of shrugged and said, "I'm thinking about asking someone, too."

"Oh really?" Nitro said in a way that showed he was surprised. "Who?"

And then I was stuck. I completely froze up for a couple of seconds, and then I opened my mouth and two words came out.

"Paula Steinmetz."

Now you might think that I had been interested in Paula for a while, and that maybe I had talked to her a couple of times after school, and that's why I said her name.

It's a fact: up to this point in time, I had never spoken to her, I mean just me and her.

Perhaps you might think that I had heard Paula sing a solo in the St. Luke's choir and had been smitten by her angelic voice. Well, she did sing in the choir and so did I, but I was over in the boys' section and couldn't hear what she sounded like. She might have been a terrible singer for all I knew. She certainly had never sung a solo.

So when Nitro asked me who I was going to ask, why did I say Paula Steinmetz?

I have no earthly idea.

When I asked her—which was another big ordeal for me, not quite up there with Luxembourg, but pretty close—Paula said yes.

She and I went skating that one time for about forty minutes and held hands for a total of about five minutes while we each tried to go backwards—a pretty smooth move if I say so myself.

And that was my one and only date.

I must confess that I liked the holding hands part quite a bit, and I think that Paula liked it too because 1) she wanted to try going backwards three or four times that night, and 2) well, she just seemed to like it. At least afterwards I never had the same experience with her that I had with Terri Donnelly.

And that brings you up to the present: Mary Drummond, third-grade fiancé; Terri Donnelly, reluctant Pilgrim wife; and a pretty nice forty minutes skating with Paula Steinmetz.

So when I mentioned that I was interested in Theresa Anwar, you definitely shouldn't get your hopes up.

———

"We have time for one more question," said Mr. Phillips.

I raised my hand and asked about the church where John Donne was pastor. I asked if St. Paul's in London was St. Paul's Episcopal, like St. Luke's was really St. Luke's Episcopal. I had just figured out that when churches were called Saint this or Saint that, they could be Episcopal, Methodist, Lutheran, Greek Orthodox, Presbyterian, Catholic, or who knows.

You couldn't tell just by the name.

Mr. Phillips started out by saying that my question was really complicated and that we should all take a Smart Pill. He paused, then told us the part about the Smart Pill was a joke.

"St. Paul's in London," he explained, "was St. Paul's Catholic for a long time because for about a thousand years there was pretty much one brand of Christianity in England—every church in England was Roman Catholic. Then King Henry VIII made St. Paul's and all the other churches in England into Anglican churches. And that's what St. Paul's is today—St. Paul's Anglican.

"Now our own St. Luke's is old, but not as old as St. Paul's," Mr. Phillips continued. "St. Luke's was founded in 1720, and back then it was St. Luke's Anglican. But as you all know from history class, we fought a war against England in 1776, and it was right around then that they changed St. Luke's name to St. Luke's Episcopal.

"I know what you are thinking—but even though St. Luke's was started in 1720, the education building we are in is not that old. In fact the oldest parts of St. Luke's that exist today date to around 1850, and the classroom section that we're in was built during the sixties. The nineteen-sixties.

"However," as Mr. Phillips talked, he went over to the window and looked out at the church cemetery, "if you go out into the churchyard, and I know that all of you have been there at one time or another, you can find one or two tombstones from the 1700s and several graves of soldiers who were killed in the Revolutionary War."

I had seen the old tombstones in the graveyard behind the church. The wind and the rain had worn away the lettering so that in places you could hardly read it. Going out there used to creep me out. But now when I looked at the graves, I sometimes wondered about what kind of lives these people had lived long ago. I wondered if they had been all that different from me.

"But why, you might ask," continued Mr. Phillips. "Why was our name changed from St. Luke's Anglican to St. Luke's Episcopal?

"Well, it's sort of like during their war against Napoleon, the British stopped calling French toast "French toast." Instead every morning the English children would wake up and say, 'Mummy, can we please have some fried bread soaked in milk and eggs with butter and syrup on top?' Think about it."

The first period bell rang.

"That bell is ringing to tell us two things," Mr. Phillips said. "1) Some of you should listen more carefully because *you are missing my jokes*, and 2) it is time for everyone to take out his or her math book."

———

Mr. Phillips decided to make social studies the last period of the day, and everyone in the class had to stand up and tell the topic of his or her report. I was the last one to go, and after I announced mine, Mr. Phillips said that my subject sounded very interesting and he was looking forward to hearing what I found out about it.

Then he said, "Well, it's been real," just as the

dismissal bell was ringing.

———

As I left the St. Luke's parking lot, rather than going home I headed across the town square to the Winston Public Library.

When I was younger, one of my parents had taken Davis and me to the library every Saturday afternoon. I liked the high ceilings in the old building and its faintly musty smell. Now I often went there by myself. I knew how to use the online card catalogue and how to find a book in the stacks. Before long, I had a big mound of books on the table in front of me.

I looked up and down the titles on the tall pile: *Passport to the Unexplained, The Cloud of Unknowing, Mystery and Awe for the Millions, The ABCs of Telepathy, The Complete Illustrated Book of Wonder, The Lives of the Saints,* and *Scams From the Great Beyond.* I took notes as I leafed through the books and wrote down a few of the major ideas about mystical experiences and some stories of people who claimed they had had them.

First, I read about famous people from history

who had had mystical experiences, people like Saint Francis and Joan of Arc.

Then with some help from the librarian, I found some materials about some interesting people from history I had never heard of before, someone called Meister Eckhart and another person named Julian of Norwich.

It's a fact: I didn't fully understand what I read about these people.

Finally, I read about some bizarre people, people who tried to make spoons bend and who would talk with your dead husband for a thousand dollars. People who had been, well, just big fakes.

One passage I came across said, "A mystical experience wipes away the film of familiar from the glass of the world." I wasn't exactly sure what that meant, but I liked it and wrote it down. Did it mean that some things or people get so familiar that we don't really notice them anymore? How exactly would a mystical experience wipe the film off familiar things or people so we could see them as they really were?

Before long I had three or four pages of my notebook filled.

After a while I put my pen on the table next to the pile of books and rubbed my eyebrows. I was not exactly sure of what I was looking for, but I had a feeling that, whatever it was, I was not finding it.

I left in time to make it home before supper without checking out any of the books.

———

As I walked home, I tried to figure out what was missing in my report. Just as I turned the corner of our block, a strong wind came down with a swoosh through the bare treetops and almost knocked me over. I squinted my eyes and looked down the street. Through the swirling snow and my watering eyes, I could just barely see our house at the end of the row. I pulled the zipper on my coat up all the way and tugged my scarf tighter. Then I put my head down into the wind and tried to walk faster.

All of a sudden, a new idea—sort of an epiphany—came to me, and I stopped and stood right where I was in the middle of the sidewalk.

I know why I couldn't find what I wanted in those

books, I thought. *Every account I read about said that a mystical experience is a very personal thing and difficult to put into words. You can't fully understand it by reading a book. I am going to have to have my own mystical experience—not just read about other people's.*

Climbing up the front steps, I wondered how exactly you went about having your own mystical experience.

I also wondered what my mother was making for our proper supper.

But mostly I wondered what my parents would say about my new not-exactly-normal idea for my not-exactly-normal project.

4

An Ug and a Yuck

"Davis, have you forgotten something?" my mother asked as we sat down at the supper table. In answer to Davis's bewildered look, she made a funny bewildered look back and then smiled and pointed to her head.

"Oh yeah," said Davis and took off his baseball cap. "Our consensus."

"And I think Cathode would prefer it if you hung your cap on the back of your chair tonight." My mother opened the blessings book and set it in front of her. "I think he's more of a soccer fan than baseball."

Davis obeyed and then took my mother's hand, who took my hand. I took my father's hand, who took Davis's other hand.

Bless our hearts to find in the breaking of this
    bread,
in the sharing of this meal,
in the love around this table,
the music of heaven.

"Amen," said my mother.

"Amen," said my father, Davis, and I.

"Please pass the corn, Todd," said my father.

"Why can't we ever have hamburgers for supper?" asked Davis as our mother put a spoonful of tuna casserole on his plate.

"We just had hamburgers Monday. Red meat once a week." This was something our mother always said. "Red meat once a week" didn't exactly rhyme, but it almost did, and I found myself saying it under my breath sometimes when I picked out lunch in the St. Luke's food line.

Lately I had found myself repeating a lot of

things my mother had said, and I wondered about it. Like what she had said about Leda—sometimes we just don't know what someone else is going through. How did these things just seem to come into my head from out of nowhere?

"We should be more thankful for what we have." Our mom said this a lot, too, and I knew she really meant it. This was another of her sayings that kept repeating in my brain.

"I try to be thankful," said Davis. "But it's much more challenging when peas are involved."

"Pick out the peas. That's what I did when I was a young lad," said my father.

"Can I, Mom?"

My mother pretended to give my father *the look* and to sigh deeply. "Just this once."

"Can I give them to Cathode?" asked Davis. "Peas are his favorite."

"And how would you know?" My mom made her eyebrows go up and down.

"Pass the rolls please, Todd," said my father. "How are the Superheroes coming along, Davis?"

"I thought up one more during school today—

73

Abacus the Human Calculator. That makes four. I only need three more."

"Good. And how did your research on mystical experiences go, Todd?"

"I found a lot of books with information about a lot of people from the past. It was good, but, well, I decided that I need more than that. A mystical experience is hard to put into words. You can know a lot about them, but not really understand them. I decided I need to have my own mystical experience and then write my report on it."

"You decided you need what?" asked my mother. Then she turned to Davis. "Cathode can eat the peas. You eat the rest."

"Well, I figure the only way I can really write about a mystical experience is to have one myself. That's kind of what the "experience" part is all about, I think."

"Hmmm. That's an interesting idea, Todd," my father said. "What do you plan to do?"

"Well, one of the books I looked at said mystical events are going on around us all the time, but we don't notice them because we're too busy. It's like we're not tuned in to them. All we need to do is try and watch for them. Our reports are due next Monday, the last day of school before Christmas break. Today is Thursday, so I've got ten days to have my mystical experience and then write about it."

"Are you going to start being different people like Leda?" asked Davis.

"No, that's not the only kind of mystical experience."

"Why do you feel you need to have a mystical experience?" my mother asked. "Is there something wrong at school? Are you unhappy about something? What about your imports and exports idea?"

"Well, sure I'm happy, Mom . . . "

"It sounds like a pretty good idea, Todd," my father said in a little more serious voice. "And after you have your experience, if you want to talk to us about it, your mother and I will be very glad to talk with you. And if you don't want to talk about it, that will be fine, too. Is that okay with you, Emma?"

"Of course that's fine," replied my mother. "In fact it sounds like a very interesting idea. Todd, you know that you don't have to always be exactly like us or always make the same choices that your father or I would. How boring that would be! Do you know that we are always proud of you?"

"Yeah, I know."

I did not do much the rest of the evening. I wanted to let everything I had read settle for a day before I started watching for my mystical experience. I helped Davis design a costume for Abacus the Human Calculator, took Cathode out for his nightly walk, watched *Don't Send a Boy to Do a Monster's Job* with my dad and Davis, and then went to bed.

The next day was Friday, and everyone had to give a progress report in social studies, which Mr. Phillips decided should be first period. Leda, or rather "Jana Cavewoman," as she now called herself, did not seem too happy when I announced that I had done some research and had decided to have my own mystical experience. At least that's the way I interpreted it. Luckily for me, Jana Cavewoman was, for the most part, only saying one word that day.

"Ug!" she said and beat on her desk with the stick she had brought in from the schoolyard. Again Mr. Phillips didn't appear to notice anything different. I wondered if this was because 1) Mr. Phillips just wanted to let Leda be Leda—or in this case Jana, or 2) because he really didn't notice anything different, which, you had to admit, was certainly a possibility.

All the rest of the day, I tried to be on the watch for a mystical experience—during school, going home, eating supper. But as far as I could tell, none took place. I did find myself noticing things more—the blue sky seemed bluer somehow, and supper tasted, well, tastier—but except for this I didn't experience anything that I would call particularly mystical.

Since it was not a school night, Davis's friend Ned came over to watch the Friday night double feature with him: *Monster to Monster* and *Tell It to the Monster*. I decided that I'd had enough monsters for a while and instead took Cathode for a long walk in Winston's town park, just off the town square alongside the river.

We got Cathode when he was just a puppy, and he was the kind that did not come already named. Some people might say that Cathode was one of those dogs that thinks he is a person, but the real truth is Cathode did not know what he was. Whenever we would watch television, he would always sit on the couch next to us and watch with us, but then he would also sleep with our cat in the cat's bed. Because he liked to watch television, we were thinking about calling him TV, but my dad said that to a dog it was not television but only a cathode ray tube with sound. In case you don't know, a cathode ray tube is the fancy name for the picture tube in a TV.

And that's how we came up with his name.

———

It was a warm night for December and windy. Wispy clouds blew across the moon, and the wind moved through the black tree branches of the trees, swaying the shadows on the snow. Cathode seemed less, well, less rambunctious than usual. Rather than jerking this way and that at the end of his rope as he usually did, he just walked quietly a few steps ahead of me in a way that seemed to be leading some-where.

From what my parents said, I knew that in a place like New York—where Teresa Anwar used to live—or California—where Leda used to live—a sixth grader could not walk alone, or even with his big rambunctious dog, after dark. In places like that I probably could even not walk home after school or take the garbage out by myself. Now if you're the kind of person who doesn't like to walk or hates to take out the garbage, you might think this would be a plus. But the town of Winston was safe, really safe, maybe too safe if there is such a thing.

The only criminals we had in Winston were litter-bugs, and there were not even very many of them.

When we reached the middle of the park, no one else was there. On winter nights when I walked Cath-ode, it was often totally deserted. All at once Cath-ode stopped abruptly and sat down on the snow. He looked to the left and then to the right and sniffed the air expectantly. I looked around but did not notice anything out of the ordinary. A fat, brown squirrel climbed down from a picnic table that was nearby and passed close to us. It hopped right over Cathode's tail and then continued calmly on its way unafraid.

I wondered if this was a sign of a mystical experience at hand, but then decided that it was no big deal.

It's a fact: nothing was ever afraid of Cathode.

Suddenly the breeze calmed, and the rush of the wind high above stilled. Cathode perked up his ears and looked around intensely.

"What is it, Cathode?" I asked. "Can you hear something? Is something out there?" He just whined and pawed the ground and wagged his tail.

"What, boy?" I knelt down and took Cathode's head in my hands. "Are you trying to tell me something? Just say it, fella."

The setter's big brown eyes looked deep into mine as though he had understood what I had said. Cathode drew closer. His eyes grew bigger as though he was looking right into my soul. He got even closer.

Then he licked me right on the mouth with his big wet tongue.

"Yuck!" I said, wiping my face on my sleeve.

Suddenly I was jerked to my feet by Cathode's rope, as he seemed to have decided that it was time to go home.

As Cathode's investigative sniffing yanked me down the block, I decided that this had definitely not been a mystical experience.

5

Noodling

The next day was Saturday. That meant piano lessons for Davis and me in the morning while our mother shopped at the Co-Op for proper groceries and then swimming lessons for us at the indoor pool at the YMCA in Deerfield. On the way home we always had lunch at Monster Burger.

My mom was a big proponent of swimming lessons because she had been on the swim team when she was in college. Davis and I were big proponents of Monster Burger although as our mother always pointed out, it did not serve the healthiest food in the world.

I got a phone call a few minutes after we got back.

"Ug! Ug! Ug! Ug!" said Jana Cavewoman and hung up.

"I am getting the feeling that Leda thinks she is the only one who can have a mystical experience," I said. "Or else maybe this is just her way of saying, 'Hey, how's it going?'"

It's a fact: it was hard to tell exactly what Jana or Leda was wanting to say.

—

Nitro and I had a favorite thing that we liked to do on Saturday afternoons. We would get Nitro's soccer ball and tell our parents we were going to walk over to St. Luke's to noodle.

According to Nitro, noodling was fifty percent practicing soccer and fifty percent just hanging out. Nitro liked noodling because he was good in soccer. I liked noodling because, well, because I needed the practice.

—

"All right, Todd, you're the man! Give this one all you've got!"

Nitro stood in the middle of the "net" that we had drawn with chalk on the brick wall on the side of St. Luke's. I stood a little ways back in the empty, snow-covered parking lot, took careful aim, and BAM! sent a shot towards the upper right-hand corner of the chalk-line goal.

"That one was still just a little bit wide," called Nitro after the ball hit about ten feet to the right of the goal. "Try again!"

BAM! I sent a weak shot that bounced twice on the snow and then went into Nitro's arms.

"You're still kicking just from your knee," called Nitro as he rolled the ball back. "Put your whole leg into it! Find your power! And try to put it somewhere that I'm not this time."

Find your power, find your power, I thought as I took aim.

BAM! I tried a third shot that was stronger. It did not bounce but still went straight into Nitro's arms again.

"That's better, but don't kick to me. You're

thinking that this is a pass. Kick away from me. The corners and the top of the goal are your targets. Put it around me or over me. Try again."

BAM! I sent a harder kick towards the lower left hand corner, but this one was wide too, so wide it completely missed the wall, and Nitro had to run around the building after it.

"Why don't you take a few shots?" I said as Nitro came back carrying the ball. I was feeling like I was getting nowhere, "I'll be goalie for a while."

Nitro walked quite a bit farther back from the wall than I had been. Then with the ball he began weaving around imaginary defenders as he announced the play-by-play: "Epstein has the ball. He swerves to the right! He cuts back left! Look out! He's past the last defender . . ."

BAM! Nitro put a perfect shot just inside the top left corner of the goal. It hit the wall with a loud smack and bounced back to him.

BAM! He put another winner in the lower right corner.

BAM! He put one just above my hands but still below the net line.

BAM! Another one in the top left corner.

"Okay, okay, that's enough! You're too hot for me today," I told him. "Let's do some passing for a while."

"I think that last one would have hit the post," said Nitro. "It was going a little bit wide."

"I don't think so." Nitro's shots rarely missed.

We practiced passing the ball back and forth for a while, with Nitro giving tips but trying not to make it look like he was really lots better, which was hard to do. Nitro said *we* a lot, as in "We need to work on this" or "We need to concentrate on that."

But both of us knew that *we* really meant *me*.

After we got tired of working on passing, we would switch to ball control, which was sort of like passing the ball to yourself. One of Nitro's favorite sayings was "Control is all." So at every noodling session after we had practiced shooting and passing, Nitro always had us work on ball control, and he had two drills for this.

The first was Anything Goes. This consisted of bouncing the ball to yourself off any part of the body that was allowed in soccer—mostly your knees and feet, but basically anything but your hands. The other drill was Head Onlys—kind of the same thing, but like the name suggested you could only use your head.

The goal was to do as many in a row as you could while the other person counted.

———

"Five, six—you're looking great, Todd. Bring your leg up a little straighter—whoops." One of my Anything Goes bounces ricocheted sideways off my knee and plopped into a snow pile at the side of the parking lot. As Nitro ran to retrieve it, he yelled back, "That was one of your better ones, Todd. You're really improving."

Nitro came back with the ball and brushed off the snow. "Ready?" he asked and then started his Anything Goes while I counted.

———

When we went noodling, Nitro was always better than me in everything—better in passing, better in shooting, and better in Anything Goes—everything except Head Onlys.

It's a fact: this was the one thing in soccer that I was good at.

"It's because your head is so huge!" Nitro always joked. I always said that the reason was because I became one with the ball.

It's a fact: my head was average-sized, like the rest of me.

So what was the real reason I could do so many more headers in a row than Nitro?

I have no earthly idea.

Noodling was actually a lot more tiring than you might think, and at some point in each practice session we would take a break and sit on, or sometimes sit in, the only place you could sit without going into the little kids' day-care playground. Off to the side of the parking lot, for reasons no one could really explain, there was a set of four concrete steps that went up and four steps that went down with a little square concrete platform on top and a round opening underneath.

When it was warm, we would sit on top and swing our legs over the edge. But in winter we always climbed inside the round part and sat with our knees scrunched up to our chests.

———

"So what are you going to be for Halloween next year?" Nitro asked as he bounced the ball against the round side of the tunnel wall a few inches in front of him.

This was one of our favorite topics during a noodle break. Each year there was a big Halloween party at St. Luke's, and everyone—including the teachers and the headmaster—wore a costume. Nitro liked to say that it was never too early to begin thinking about what you were going to wear. The goal was to come up with a costume that was unique and different. The trick was to not come up with something that so unique and different no one could tell what you were. Every time we talked about it, Nitro would come up with something new. He called it his Costume-of-the-Month.

I bounced the ball a few times off the other side of the tunnel. "I am thinking that I will be a hot dog."

"A hot dog," said Nitro. "That's good. No one in

class has ever been a hot dog before."

"I know." I handed Nitro the ball. "So what are you going to be?"

"I am thinking that I will be a soccer player." Nitro bounced the ball a bit.

"You were a soccer player last year."

"I know," said Nitro. "But last year I was Pele. This year I'm going to be Mia Hamm."

"Mia Hamm . . . I like that."

Nitro handed the ball back to me. "Are you thinking that you would be a hot dog in a bun or just a hot dog?"

"I haven't decided yet," I said and gave the ball a few bounces. "What do you think?"

Nitro thought about it for a moment. "I would definitely go with the hot dog in a bun, or perhaps possibly a corn dog. If you went as just a hot dog, people might think you were supposed to be a huge carrot or a giant Cheeto."

"Good point." I bounced the ball off the wall a couple more times. "So, are you really going to be Mia Hamm next year?"

"Well, probably not. But, it is a back-up, in case

I don't get a better idea. I'm worried that I would come to the Halloween party as Mia Hamm, and everyone would think I was supposed to be a Spice Girl or something."

"That would not be good."

"No, it wouldn't." Nitro looked over at me. "Well, you ready for Head Onlys?"

"Yeah, let's go."

———

"Ten, eleven, control is all, twelve . . ." Nitro counted as I bounced the ball off my head. "You do realize that the real reason that you're so great at this is because you have a gigantic head." Nitro had just done eleven Head Onlys in a row.

"I mean, I am your best friend, so I can tell you this—your head is huge! Fourteen, fifteen, sixteen . . ." Our all-time record for Head Onlys was thirty in a row, and I had set it.

"SEE . . . the . . . ball . . . BE . . . the . . . ball," I answered in between hits and out of breath.

"Eighteen, nineteen," said Nitro. "Keep going, Todd, you're going to beat your record . . . twenty-

91

one, twenty-two, rats!"

I had stumbled a little in trying to get centered under the ball, and number twenty-two careened off to the side. We watched as it landed in a snow bank.

"Well, twenty-two is awfully good," Nitro said. "Even for someone with a certain unfair advantage. Are you ready for my Famous Backwards Reverse Pass before we head home?"

"I guess so."

———

The last thing we did in every noodling session was to practice Nitro's Famous Backwards Reverse Pass five times. This was a super difficult kick that I didn't even try to do. It was so hard that Nitro couldn't even do it.

At least not yet.

Five times Nitro would stand about twenty feet away with his back turned towards me. Five times I would toss the ball up high so it would arc over Nitro's shoulder and come down right in front of him. Five times Nitro would jump up and try to kick it backwards back to me, kicking so high that he would fall down on his behind. Five times Nitro would completely miss the ball.

Each time he would announce that he was getting closer.

Once I had asked Nitro why he called it his Famous Backwards Reverse Pass, since backwards and reverse meant the same thing. Nitro had said:

"The Reverse part refers to the pass. The Backwards part refers to me."

———

"You ready for your last try?" I asked.

"Ready," said Nitro with his back to me. He had missed the ball on each of his first four attempts.

"Ready . . . Set . . . Go." I tossed the ball up into the air.

Looking over his right shoulder, Nitro watched the ball sail in. Then with careful timing, he jumped, kicked his right leg up and backward, and . . . missed, and fell down on his backside.

We watched the ball bounce a couple times, roll a little, then stop.

"You know, I think I'm getting closer. I am definitely getting closer." Nitro looked up at me from where he sat in the snow. "Well, you ready to go?"

"Yeah, I'm ready."

———

"You know what I'm thinking?" Nitro asked as we were walking out of the parking lot.

"No, what?"

"I'm thinking that I might be a giant Cheeto for Halloween next year."

I considered this for a bit. "Aren't you afraid that everyone would be coming up and asking if you were a hot dog without a bun?"

"I am thinking that I might be a round cheese puff, not a cheese curl," said Nitro.

"A cheese puff."

"Yes, a cheese puff."

"A round, orange Cheeto cheese puff," I said. "What if everyone thinks you're supposed to be a giant tangerine, or the planet Mars, or something?"

"Well," said Nitro as we turned the corner, "at least no one will think I'm a Spice Girl."

———

That night after supper, Davis went over to Ned's to spend the night, and my parents went across the street to the Johnsons' for their Occasional Saturday Night Healthy Supper Club.

"Say hello to Leda, I mean Jana, for me," I said.

"Ug! Ug!" said my father as he grabbed his coat.

"Come on, Neanderthal Man, we're going to be late," said my mother pulling him out the door.

After everyone had left, I made popcorn and watched *No Monsters Need Apply*. I liked it sometimes when I could watch a scary movie alone, although alone really meant with Cathode. During commercials, I made trails of popcorn for Cathode to follow, sometimes circles, sometimes figure 8s or Christmas trees, or some other pattern. I tried to work it so that Cathode reached the last piece of popcorn in the trail and would jump back on the couch with me just as the movie started again.

After the movie was over, I practiced a few songs on the piano from the Christmas book. I liked playing when no one else could hear. Then I put Cathode out on the porch, took out the garbage, and went to bed.

"A Gallery of Seven Superheroes by Davis Farrel" was spread across my brother's desk. I turned out the light and crawled under the covers. Then I remembered my social studies report and decided to try an experiment.

I thought of my best friend and tried to communicate with him.

"*TODD CALLING NITRO. TODD CALLING NITRO. COME IN, NITRO.*"

In my mind, I conjured up an image of Nitro at his favorite hobby: making rockets. In my mind, I saw Nitro at his workbench. There were hundreds of rolls of red paper caps piled next to him, but instead of putting them into a toy gun and shooting them, Nitro was scraping the black powder from each little cap into a cardboard tube that had red fins glued on the bottom and a pointed cone on the top.

"*NITRO, DO YOU READ ME? OVER.*"

Nothing. I tried to think of a message I could send. All I could think of was a song. I tried to send the words across town to Nitro's house:

"*CITY SIDEWALKS BUSY SIDEWALKS DRESSED IN HOLIDAY STYLE STOP IN THE AIR*

THERE'S A FEELING OF CHRISTMAS STOP SILVER BELLS SILVER BELLS IT'S CHRISTMAS TIME IN THE CITY STOP HEAR THEM RING STOP RING-A-LING STOP SOON IT WILL BE CHRISTMAS DAY OVER."

I looked at the clock. It was nine twenty-nine. Too early really to go to sleep on a Friday night, but almost too late to, well, our parents had a consensus about not calling friends after nine-thirty. I decided to make a very quick call to Nitro to see if he had gotten the message. The phone rang three times, and then Nitro's mother answered.

"Hello, Mrs. Epstein. This is Todd. Is Alex there?"

"Yes, hold on, Todd . . . Alex, telephone."

"Hello?"

"Hey, Nitro. This is Todd."

"Hi ya, Todd. What's up?"

"Nitro, I want you to think very carefully, all right?"

"Okay."

"Do the words 'silver bells' mean anything to you?"

97

"Silver bells?"

"Right."

"Hmm . . . Is this a riddle or something?"

"No. I just want to know if the words 'silver bells' mean anything to you."

"I don't think so."

"How about 'city sidewalks'?"

"City sidewalks . . . silver bells . . . Are you writing a poem?"

"No! I'm working on my report for social studies."

"Well, those words don't mean anything to me."

"Rats. Hey, you weren't making a rocket with the black powder from caps and a cardboard tube when I called, were you?"

"No, I was finishing a game of Chinese checkers with Hannah Louise. But that sounds like a pretty neat idea." Hannah Louise was Nitro's little sister. She was in the same class as Davis at St. Luke's. "What are you up to anyway?"

"I'm trying to have my mystical experience, but it's not going too well."

"Well, you'd better get going. You only have one

more week. It's due a week from Monday."

"I know. What'd you say you're doing your report on?"

"The decriminalization of firecrackers."

"Oh yeah, you told me. Well, thanks for trying to help, Nitro. See you in school."

"School—don't remind me. Anyway, you're welcome. Remember, you're the man."

"Yeah, right. Bye, Nitro."

We hung up, and I went back to bed. *Another failure at having a mystical experience,* I thought. *Oh well, I can always go back to imports and exports.* Soon I was asleep.

———

Very late in the night, I had a dream. In my dream I saw Nitro again, working on his rockets.

"This is going to be a big one," said Nitro.

Then there was a loud explosion and a bright flash. When the smoke cleared, Asbestos the Human Torch was standing where Nitro had been.

"Nitro!" I exclaimed. "You are Asbestos's secret identity!"

99

"That's right, Todd," Asbestos said in a rich, deep voice. "I know I can count on you to keep my secret. My work here is done. Bye now."

Asbestos pushed the fire bomb button on his belt and disappeared in a blaze of flames. Then the scene changed a little, and from the flames there arose a giant monster that resembled a dragon. With a flap of its big black wings, the monster flew up into the air and circled around a city that looked a lot like Tokyo. It belched fire and thick gray smoke from its mouth, and from every belch there sprang up another fiery monster until the Asian sky was full of flying creatures of various sizes and shapes.

I yelled and woke up.

"Whew! What a dream!" I opened my eyes and looked around. It was still dark out. I was hot and thirsty and went downstairs to get a drink. The water from the kitchen faucet tasted especially cool and refreshing. Outside the kitchen window a few stars stood out in the late night sky. I did not feel sleepy at all, so I decided to go and lie on the couch in the living room instead of going back up to bed. This was something that I did every so often.

It's a fact: if you wake up and can't get back to sleep, moving to the couch always helps.

I found my way over to the sofa and turned on the end table lamp. It was cold downstairs, so I wrapped up in the afghan that my grandmother had knitted and looked over a pile of books and magazines that my parents had sitting out.

I leafed through *Reader's Digest* and *Golf Digest*. Then I looked through the articles in *Food Digest*, one of my mother's cooking magazines. As I turned the pages, I found:

"How to Cook Everything on a Stick!"

"Soybean Sandwiches"

"Blender Power!—Making Shakes with Nutritious Foods"

"Tell Them It's Chicken—Getting Your Family to Try New Foods"

My father's Bible was open, like it often was on Saturday evenings, to the readings for church the next day. I looked at the passage my father had marked. It said:

"Enter by the narrow gate. For wide is the gate, and broad the way, that leads to destruction, and those who enter by it are many."

What does that mean? I wondered. *Does it mean that it's hard to get to heaven? Does it mean most people won't go to heaven? Why would God make it hard? Why shouldn't the way to heaven be the broad way?*

I sighed and decided maybe I asked too many questions and maybe this was not what the passage meant at all. Perhaps this was another one of those things that I would understand when I was older. I hoped Pastor Jill would be speaking that morning. She usually explained things so they made sense.

Thinking these thoughts, I fell asleep on the couch.

When I woke up, sunlight was shining in through the window, and from the sounds coming from the kitchen, it was clear that my father was in charge of making a proper breakfast for everyone before we went to church. Soon my father's call and the smell of sizzling fried bread soaked in milk and eggs told me it was time to get up.

6

The Extraordinary Ordinary

If you went to St. Luke's the church—which, you could say, was quite traditional in a lot of ways—you did a lot of things exactly the same each Sunday.

You said a lot of the same words and prayed a lot of the same prayers. Some people wore the same clothes every week, and even sat in the same spot. I usually did not like it when something was the always the same every time, but church was different. The sameness each week made church seem friendly, and familiar, and a little, well, mystical.

I can't explain why.

St. Luke's the church always began with the

same words:

The Lord be with you.
And also with you.

"When I was growing up, all my brothers were on our high school's wrestling team," Pastor Jill told the congregation as she stood in the pulpit and began her sermon. Her short brown hair was straight, and her bangs came down over her brown glasses. When she spoke at church, over her clothes she wore a long black robe that looked like the gowns the eighth graders wore when they graduated, only hers was nicer and fancier, and seemed to suit her. I thought that it made her look, well, interesting, but I would never say this to anyone except maybe Nitro. I noticed for the first time that Pastor Jill was only about as tall as an eighth grader.

"So I learned how to be a pretty good wrestler myself. And even though he is almost six feet tall, I can still pin my husband when I really want to." She stopped a moment and looked around as if to say, "Think about that!"

"Sometimes, though, I find myself wrestling with God, and let me tell you that when I do, I never win. I think that many people wrestle with God about the passage that we heard earlier for today's reading.

"Many people wonder if the part about the narrow gate refers to heaven. But when I read this passage, I think about our life on earth.

"How hard it is to accept the love that God has for each of us." Pastor Jill paused to let this sink in. "How hard it is to see the everyday grace that surrounds us. How hard it is to see people who differ from us as our brothers and our sisters.

"How easy it is for me to miss the good that is in each moment. How easy it is for me to label people who are different as wrong, and how easy to label myself as right. How easy it is to miss the ordinary miracles that are going on all the time."

I especially liked this last part and got a pencil from my mother and wrote it down in case I wanted to use it in my report: *How easy it is to miss the ordinary miracles that are going on all the time.*

"We call this time of year we are in, the four weeks that come before Christmas, the season of

Advent." Pastor Jill reached under the pulpit and brought out a dictionary and opened it to her book-mark.

"Advent," she read. "Something that is coming into being." She closed the dictionary and put it back.

"But I think the best way to remember what Advent means is to think of the line from the song 'Joy to the World' that goes like this:

Let ev-ery hear-rt
Prepar-re hi-im ro-o-om. . . .

Pastor Jill sang the line in a high clear voice, and the last note echoed around the sanctuary and faded out.

And that was the end of her sermon.

———

The next day at school was Monday, one week from when our reports were due.

"For morning reflections today I want to talk about two words," said Mr. Phillips as he grabbed his

106

blue marker, his second favorite color and the one he used when he wanted something to stand out.

"Extraordinary — Ordinary," he said as he put the words on the board. "Let's take the first one first." Mr. Phillips picked up his big dictionary.

"Extraordinary: going beyond what is usual, something beyond what is normal."

Then he looked up to the second word. "Ordinary: something that is customary, unexceptional, common."

"These words seem to be opposites, don't they? But what if we take out the dash between them?" Mr. Phillips erased the dash from the board. "What if we talk about the Extraordinary Ordinary?"

"Those who brought your lunch today, I would like for you to open your lunch bags or lunch boxes and take out everything and put it on your desk." Mr. Phillips waited a moment as those with lunches, about half the class, started pulling out food of all sorts.

"Now who in class has the most ordinary thing to eat?"

Nitro held up an apple. "How about this?"

"Yes, that's good. We might think that an apple is not very special. Who else besides Alex has something that seems ordinary in his or her lunch?"

"What about this?" David Minstro held up his sandwich.

Mr. Phillips walked over to David's desk and took a closer look. "Two pieces of plain white bread with peanut butter. Creamy, I believe. Yes, that's good too. We might think of creamy peanut butter on white bread as very ordinary. Does anyone have anything even more ordinary than this?"

Leda held up a small bag. "What about this?" Leda had gone back to being regular Leda, at least for that day, if there was such as thing as regular Leda.

Mr. Phillips went over to Leda's desk to inspect. "A baggie of dry shredded mini-wheat squares," he announced and held the baggie up for everyone to take a look at and then handed it back to Leda. "No milk. No sugar. Not even frosted mini-wheats. Just dry shredded wheat squares. Could there be any food more ordinary than this?"

"Actually, I quite enjoy them," said Leda in a

108

voice that Mr. Phillips wasn't exactly supposed to hear.

"Precisely!" said Mr. Phillips. "And if you were hungry, and if your plane had crashed, and you were castaway on a desert island with nothing to eat but coconuts for weeks and weeks, and if a baggie of dry shredded wheat squares washed ashore on the tide one day, you would take that baggie in your hand, and you would hold it up to the skies. And then you would say, 'This is a *miracle!*' You would say, 'This is *amazing!*'"

Mr. Phillips turned to Leda. "May I try one?" Leda took out one dry shredded mini-wheat from the baggie, and Mr. Phillips popped it into his mouth.

"You would declare, 'This is *extraordinary!*'" Mr. Phillips said as he crunched with delight.

He swallowed and went on. "Now I want everyone to look at the clock, and when I say go, I want each one of you to take a deep breath and hold it as long as you can. Everyone ready to hold your breath? Ready . . . set . . . go!"

We all took a deep breath and watched the second hand on the clock as it slowly moved past each number.

"Fifteen seconds," said Mr. Phillips in a funny voice that said that he was holding his breath too. "Thirty seconds." A few students let out their breaths. "Forty-five seconds." One by one students were letting out their breath with big whooshes.

"One minute five seconds." I let out my breath, and Mr. Phillips exhaled loudly a few seconds after me. Soon there were only two students who had not breathed—Leda and Nitro.

"One minute fifteen seconds . . . One minute twenty seconds . . ." Leda let out her breath with a big gasp.

"One minute twenty-five seconds." Still Nitro held out. "One minute thirty seconds . . . One minute forty seconds . . . One minute fifty seconds . . ." Nitro finally breathed out a huge breath and then huffed and puffed really hard and fast about ten times.

"The air that covers Earth has been around a long, long time," Mr. Phillips went on over Nitro's gasps. "It has been breathed in and out by countless generations of people and trees, birds and fish, and mosquitoes and elephants.

"The air over Winston may have once been over London, or even the South Pole. The air you are breathing today may have been breathed by the first students at St. Luke's, by people who fought in the Revolutionary War, or even by John Donne." Mr. Phillips paused and gave us the look that said, 'Give that some thought!'

"And each time you exhale, you send out a little bit of yourself that will always exist.

"A breath of air," Mr. Phillips continued. "You can't find anything more ordinary. We breathe all day long and never think what a miracle it is. We never see a breath of air as something amazing. We never take a breath and say, 'Wow! This is *extraordinary!*'"

Mr. Phillips stopped for one of his let-it-sink-in moments.

"The Extraordinary Ordinary. Something to think about, isn't it?" He looked around and didn't say anything, and then we understood that this had been a rhetorical question.

"All right, thank you very much," Mr. Phillips went on. "You may put your apples and your peanut butter sandwiches and your shredded wheat squares

111

away and take out your English books."

Something to think about, isn't it? I couldn't decide what I thought about the Extraordinary Ordinary. Did it mean that all the things that seemed, well, so everyday, were actually quite special? Or did it mean that special things were happening all the time, every day? Just when I thought that I had grasped what Mr. Phillips was saying, I lost it again. As I got out my English book, I decided that I would have to think more about it later.

For half the period we went over the story we had been reading. Then Mr. Philips told us to take out a piece of paper and a pen. For some assignments he let us use a pencil or a pen. For math problems we had to use a pencil. But when he said we must take out a pen it meant one thing: an in-class writing assignment.

I did not hate in-class writing assignments, but it's a fact: I did not love them either. The writing part was fine, but deciding what to write on was always a problem for me.

"We have been reading about heroes for the past three weeks," Mr. Phillips said. "Now it's time for you to write something about them. Sometimes I ask you to write about a very specific thing, but today I am giving you a choice of topics. Your assignment today is to write about something that has to do with a hero or heroes. If you write about heroes, remember that you make the plural of hero by adding e-s."

Another decision about what to write about, I thought, another chance to do something different from what I normally do, or else just to do something normal again.

"You can write about your favorite hero or heroes from the ones that we read about," Mr. Phillips continued, saying the z sound at the end of "heroes" very carefully. "You can write about a living hero in your own life. You can define what a hero is. You can write about a famous person who is a hero. You can tell who your own heroes are. You must write for twenty minutes. No more, and no less. And you may not talk. Beginning now!"

For an extraordinary teacher, you could say that Mr. Phillips was quite traditional when it came to in-class writing. When he said—"You must write for twenty minutes. No more, and no less. And you may not talk"—he meant it. The only sound for twenty minutes was the sound of twenty pens on twenty pieces of paper.

Well, nineteen. I stared at my blank sheet of paper, and thought, and chewed on my pen, and rubbed my eyebrows. Finally I got an idea.

I AM NOT A HERO
by Todd Farrel

I am not a hero.

For the past three weeks we have read about heroes in English class. These heroes were all people who did something extraordinary. I cannot ride the horse that no one else can ride. I cannot catch spies or fly around on a special cool broomstick, or defeat the evil villain.

What can I do? I can play the piano okay, and I can swim pretty well, but that is only because my mom makes us take lessons. I can also write pretty well, if I can find a topic.

The heroes in books make everything they do look easy. It seems like they were already born with their special abilities and never had to work at it. I try to swim some extra laps each week while my brother's class is finishing, and I'm supposed to practice piano for 20 minutes every day, but I don't always do it.

I am not a hero. Heroes are people who do something special for other people. I pick up my dirty dishes and take out the garbage, and my mom doesn't have to ask me each time. I shovel the sidewalk with my dad. I help my little brother with his homework sometimes. This does not make me a hero.

A hero would be someone who saves the whole city or even saves one person. A hero is someone who is really brave. That is not me. My idea of an adventure is if I watch a scary movie by myself, and by myself really means with our dog. I like my adventures to

115

be only a little scary.

I am not a hero. A hero is someone who does something really difficult, something so hard that they couldn't do it without some kind of super power. A hero is someone found in books, someone who is different from everyone else.

Do I know any real heroes?

Maybe, but I will have to think about this some more.

This last sentence was my way to end an in-class writing when I still had more time but no more ideas. And Mr. Phillips always liked it if you said that you were going to think about something.

After exactly twenty minutes—no more and no less—Mr. Phillips collected our papers and told everyone that he looked forward to reading what we had to say.

7

Synchronicity

"A person who asks an honest question praises God."

It looked like Tuesday's morning reflections were going to be Question Time again.

"Last night, I had a sudden perception," Mr. Phillips continued. "I had the striking insight that we might need to have Question Time again for morning reflections during homeroom. I had an epiphany that there still might be someone with a question he or she would like to ask. Who would like to start?"

Nitro's hand shot up. "I have a question. Why do we call homeroom 'homeroom' when except for the parking lot and the lunchroom we never go anywhere else? At Curtis Winston they have homeroom, but they have a different room for science, a different room for math, a different room for everything."

Mr. Phillips wrote the word "homeroom" on the marker board. Then he acted as if he was looking the word up in his dictionary. I wasn't really sure that it was in the dictionary.

"Homeroom," Mr. Phillips pretended to read. "A classroom that students report to, especially at the beginning of the day."

"Homeroom," he went on. "A room with a home-like feeling, a place where students feel they all belong, where everyone feels like a big family."

"Another way to approach your question, Alex," said Mr. Phillips as he closed his dictionary and put it back on the desk, "another way to understand why little St. Luke's calls each grade's only classroom its homeroom, is to ask yourself—Why do they call ice-covered Greenland, Greenland? Think about it. . . . Now, does anyone else have a question for us to ponder?"

Leda raised her hand. "If being yourself, like

118

being different, is good, then why do we have a dress code and all have to wear the same thing? They don't have a dress code . . ."

"At Curtis Winston?" said Mr. Phillips.

"I was going to say, they don't have a dress code at the school I went to in California."

"Ah, the St. Luke's dress code question." Mr. Phillips paused a moment and then said, "If you want our dress code to make sense, you can approach it from several directions, and it's a little complicated, so begin by taking not one, but two Smart Pills.

"One way to tell if something is important to us is by what we wear. Weddings are important, so people dress up. Funerals are important, so people dress up. If you came to someone's wedding or someone's funeral in dirty clothes, or sloppy clothes, or even just the clothes that you wear after school to play in, you might give them the impression that you didn't think their wedding or funeral was very important. So when we all dress up to come to school, we are showing that the learning we do here is important. That's one way to understand our dress code.

"The second reason for having a dress code is

119

easy to see. As I stand in front of class each day, I can tell when you're not tuning in to what I'm saying—*especially when you miss my jokes.* Having a dress code gives you one less thing to be distracted by and helps you to stay focused, so you can laugh at the proper times. That's a joke.

"A third way to think about the dress code is to think that while many times differences can be good, sometimes being different can be a bad thing." Mr. Phillips paused and looked as though he was remembering something from a long time ago.

"In schools without dress codes," he went on, "students who come from wealthy families can wear expensive clothes, but many families can't afford to buy the popular brands for their kids. You might think that not having a dress code would be great, but what if everyone in class wore really expensive, cool clothes except you? How would you feel?

"What if you were the girl who always had to wear the same old skirt every day? What if you were the boy whose only pair of shoes came from The Red Shutter?"

The Red Shutter was the store in Winston that

sold used clothing and other used stuff like beat-up toasters and dishes that didn't match. It was a place that, well, not everyone who went there was poor, but a lot were.

"Put yourself in that boy's shoes. Would you like being different from everyone else if you were him?" Mr. Phillips took another of his famous sink-in pauses.

"That, young men and young women, is a rhetorical question. And that is all the time we have for Question Time this morning, so please take out your math books."

Would you like being different? I thought. *Would I like being different?*

———

Mr. Phillips was fond of saying that it was never too early to begin practicing for the annual sixth grade soccer match against Winston Elementary that was held every June, especially since St. Luke's had never won. So for P.E. that day, our class was once again divided into two teams for snow soccer, which was played out on the snow-packed parking lot.

121

Mr. Phillips made David Minstro the goalie for one team, and Leda Johnson the other. Mr. Phillips always chose Leda to be one of the two goalies, and no one ever complained. For one thing, she could kick farther than anyone else in class, including Nitro. And for another, few shots got past her. Very few.

It's a fact: the rest of the class was looking to Nitro and Leda to keep our team from falling apart in the game against Curtis Winston, like those fancy toothpicks they stick in sandwiches with too many fillings — Nitro and Leda being the fancy toothpicks and the rest of us being the falling-apart sandwich.

Leda had worn little Christmas bells in her shoe-laces that day, and every time she kicked the ball, they jingled.

———

"One minute left!" called Mr. Phillips in a voice that sounded funny because he had his whistle grasped between his teeth. The game had been a hard-fought one, and the score was still tied zero to zero.

From my place far up-field in the parking lot, I saw Theresa Anwar suddenly break free from a group of defenders. With her long black hair flying behind her, BAM! she blasted the ball at Leda's goal with a shot that was going right for the lower corner!

Leda dove hard to her left and slid across the snow. With her longs arms and fingers outstretched as far as she could reach, she caught the ball at the very last instant just before it would have crossed the net! Then Leda jumped back up, took two steps, and BAM!—kicked the ball high into the air, dropping it deep to Nitro.

"Take it to the net, Nitro!" Leda called. "It's time to create some havoc down there, Alex baby!"

Jingle-ling-a-ling went her shoes.

Nitro settled the ball and quickly started moving downfield. If Leda was our best goalie, Nitro was the best in the field and always scored the most. He faked and dribbled around one defender while I ran up along the other sideline. Nitro sent a perfect pass across the field that bounced right in front of me. I got control of it, got around one defender who slipped and fell, and headed for the net. Nitro, who was also the fastest runner in class, had streaked up and had gotten into position in case my shot got blocked.

Together we flanked opposite sides of the goal with no one between us and the net except David Minstro.

"Take the shot!" Nitro yelled. For a moment, I thought I should try to score, but then I changed my mind and passed the ball back to Nitro.

David slid over to guard Nitro's side of the net. Nitro let the ball bounce once and then immediately passed it back to me.

"TAKE THE SHOT!" Nitro yelled again.

The other team's defenders had recovered and were almost upon us. I hesitated a fraction of a second and then slammed my foot into the ball. It sailed up into the air towards the goal but was veering just a bit wide and was going to miss.

In a flash, Nitro was under it. Looking over his right shoulder as he ran, Nitro watched the ball descend. Then with careful timing, he jumped, kicked his right leg up and backward, and . . . did not miss ! Catching the ball in mid-air with his foot, Nitro sent the ball back to me with a gentle, perfect Famous

Backwards Reverse Pass. The ball soared into the sky and was curving down right where I was positioned in front of the goal.

"Head it, Todd!" Nitro shouted from where he was sprawled backside on the snow. "HEAD IT!!!"

The ball seemed to float as it came downwards, and everything around me slowed down in a way that was, well, kind of mystical. As I jumped up to head it, the words *BE . . . THE . . . BALL . . .* went through my mind. And it may sound bizarre, but at that moment I knew exactly what was going to happen, as though I could already see it.

In that instant I banged my head into the ball, sending it around David's outstretched arms and into the net for a score!

Nitro leapt up and ran over to me and first gave me a huge double high-five, and then he just sort of jumped on top of me and keep beating me on the back. In a voice that only I could hear, he said, "See? I knew you could do it!" With his big smile he added in the same low voice, "With *your* head, how could you miss!"

Suddenly the whole team was there giving us

both high-fives, and I was caught up in a wonderful whirling, slapping hands with everyone and being congratulated.

Then Mr. Phillips' whistle blew. "Time's up! Lunch period, everyone! The Chrysanthemums win—one to nothing!"

It's a fact: Mr. Phillips always gave weird names to the teams in our class.

———

As the sixth grade snow soccer players scurried inside, David Minstro caught up with me.

"Sweet header, Todd," said David with a genuine smile. Everyone knew I was not one of the big scorers in the class.

"Yes, that was a very nice shot today, Todd," said Mr. Phillips who suddenly appeared walking behind us. "A very nice shot."

Then Mr. Phillips looked over at Nitro who was walking next to me. In a quieter, serious voice he continued, "And those were excellent passes, Alex. Excellent. All three of them. And I don't mean just your Famous Backwards Reverse Pass. Do you hear what I'm saying?"

"Thanks," Nitro answered, proud but also a little embarrassed at being the focus of Mr. Phillips' praise. "I mean, yes, sir."

"You both remember this. Understand?"

"Yes, sir," we said together.

"All right. I have to go see if my wife brought us anything extraordinary to eat today. I'll see you back in class after lunch." Mr. Phillips disappeared through the door into the teachers' lounge.

As we headed down the hallway, I looked over and caught Nitro's eye. I nodded to him. He nodded back. No words were necessary. We both knew what had taken place during the final thirty seconds of snow soccer that day.

Nitro had given up his opportunity to be the hero so I could be one.

———

On Tuesdays Nitro always brought his lunch because on Tuesdays he always ate in Mrs. Allbright's room with the St. Luke's Rocket Club. On Tuesdays I always bought my lunch, because Tuesday at St.

127

Luke's was pizza day. So Nitro told me one more time what a great shot it was, and I told him one more time what a great Famous Backwards Reverse Pass it was, and then he took off.

As I was coming out of the lunch line with my carton of chocolate milk and two slices of pizza, I saw that Leda was sitting off in one corner of the lunchroom sort of by herself.

That was good, because today I needed to talk to her sort of alone.

I took a deep breath and walked over to where she was.

I set down my tray across from Leda and looked down at my pizza and chocolate milk. Leda's tray looked like the produce section at the Co-op. She had an orange, an apple, a bunch of grapes, a banana, a baggie filled with whole wheat crackers, and a carton of skim milk. I took out a folded-up piece of paper from my pocket. Just for a second, the light hit her long, blond hair just right, and there was her nice shimmery flash. I pulled out my chair and sat down.

"Nice saves today, Leda," I said. "Especially on that last shot Theresa kicked."

"Thanks, Todd. That was an astounding header you made," said Leda. "And how about Nitro's remarkable pass? He looked like Mia Hamm out there."

"Do you think I could ask you some questions about mystical experiences?"

"It would be my pleasure."

I opened up the list of questions I had written the night before and began. "Number One. Do you think that everyone can have a mystical experience?"

"Yes."

I got out my pencil and wrote *yes* down carefully.

"Question Number Two has two parts. Part A: Do you think that everyone is more than one person? And part B: If yes, can you give an example?"

"Part A: Yes, I think that each person can be many different people," Leda answered. "Part B: For example, even though I am the same person, I am one Leda at school, I am a completely different Leda at home, and I am a third Leda at church. Part B another example: When I was little and lived in California, I was one person. Now I am another. And when I am grown up I will be a third."

I liked that answer and wrote it down carefully, too.

Leda continued, "Some famous person, I don't remember who, once said that a rose would smell just as sweet, no matter what it was called, but I think names can be of great consequence sometimes. My real name's not Leda, you know. It's Aletha. So when I'm older and a different person, like when I'm a teen-ager, maybe I'll go by my full name."

I thought about that for a moment then went on. "Question Number Three. How does a person know if they have really had a mystical experience?"

"Well," said Leda and she paused. "Well, perhaps not everyone who says they have had a mystical experience has really had one. I have been thinking that there is one way you can tell for certain—it will leave you better than before."

It will leave you better than before. Another good answer. I wrote it down.

"That's all my regular questions, except for Question Number Four, which is this: Do you have anything else that you would like to say?"

"Yes, I do," Leda answered. "I would like to say thank you for your questions, and I would also like to thank you very much for having lunch with me. This has been splendid."

"It was, well, my pleasure," I replied.

And then we both just ate our lunches. Leda gave me one of her mini-wheat squares to try, and I told her it was not bad, which was the truth.

And that was the end of lunch period.

———

"Hello, everybody!"

I turned around. Pastor Jill was standing in the doorway in the back of the class.

A classroom visit from Pastor Jill was a rare experience. Unless they went to church, students usually saw her only at school chapel on Wednesdays. Pastor Jill was taller than most of the sixth graders, but not by much. Besides being kind of short for an adult, she was also thin. I didn't see how she could really be all that strong, but Mr. Phillips had told us that it was a fact: he always lost to her when they wrestled.

"Has anyone seen Tim?" she asked the class.

Tim? Who's Tim? I thought. *There's no one in class named Tim.*

"I'm over here, Babe." Mr. Phillips crawled out from under his desk where he had dropped one of his markers. "Class, we have a very special guest today," he announced as he stood up. "For anyone who has not already met her personally, this is my wife, Jill. She asked me if she could talk to you for the last five minutes of school today about the Christmas concert coming up this Friday."

Pastor Jill walked to the front of the class and began saying something about the concert, but I didn't hear it because I was still in shock.

Mr. Phillips is TIM? And Pastor Jill is BABE? Maybe Leda was really right. Maybe you can be one person at school, and another person at church, and another person at home. Babe and Tim. Wow!

". . . and so this year we want to try something new," continued Pastor Jill as I tuned back in to what she was saying.

"We want to bring back Boxing Day! So we are asking every student who comes to the concert to bring a gift with them. Something that we can give either to the special people who serve St. Luke's every day—like our janitors or our cooks—or something that we can give to the needy in our area.

"What you bring is entirely up to you. We will put all the gifts under the Christmas tree, and then on Boxing Day, December 26th, we will deliver them. Some will go to the families of our staff, some we will take to The Red Shutter, and any food gifts we will bring to God's Pantry in Deerfield.

"Does anyone have any questions they would like to ask about the concert or Boxing Day, or since we have some time left, any questions they would like to ask me about anything else?"

There was a pause, and then Theresa Anwar raised her hand and gave one of her room-brightening smiles. "Do you know what you are going to get Mr. Phillips for Christmas?"

"Yes, I do, but let me warn you that it's a little complicated, so everyone needs to take a Smart Pill," Pastor Jill said. Then she launched into the story about their not buying each other presents so they could take the ski trip to Vermont over spring break.

". . . Of course, I will probably get Mr. Phillips something small for Christmas morning, so I was wondering if you had any suggestions. He thinks he's going to get a book or a CD, but you know, I have been thinking about maybe getting him a tie! What do you think?"

"That, I believe, is my wife's idea of a joke," said Mr. Phillips jumping in.

Suddenly the final bell rang.

"Oops, we're out of time," finished Pastor Jill. "I look forward to seeing you and your families at the concert—Friday night at seven-thirty. And don't forget about Boxing Day! And one last thing . . ." Pastor Jill smiled and looked around at us. "It's been real."

———

After school, I went to choir practice for Friday's concert. First we worked on "O Come, O Come Emmanuel." It had a sad sense to it that gave me a lonesome feeling, but one that Leda might have said was a splendid lonesome feeling.

Then we practiced "Good King Wenceslas." As

I sang the words, all at once I had an epiphany, and I stopped singing right then and there. I realized for the first time that it was a song about a mystical experience!

I wondered if this was an example of synchronicity—the word my dad had talked about.

Good King Wenceslas looked out
  on the feast of Stephen . . .

Good King Wenceslas looked outside his castle and saw a poor man trying to gather firewood in the snow. It happened to be the Feast of Stephen, a day which the choir director told us was celebrated on the same day as Boxing Day in Great Britain, a day to help people in need.

The king felt sorry for the man and asked his page to help him bring some food and some wood to the poor man's cottage, and off they set. As they went, it got darker and darker and colder and colder. Soon the page couldn't go any farther.

Sire, the night is darker now,

and the wind blows stronger.
Fails my heart, I know not how,
I can go no longer . . .

Just when the page thought he would not be able to make it one more step, he called out for help, and King Wenceslas said to him:

Mark my footsteps, my good page,
tread thou in them boldly.
Thou shalt find the winter's rage
freeze thy blood less coldly.

As the page began walking in the steps the king had left in the snow, heat began to mysteriously come up out of the ground to warm him, and so they were able to reach the poor man's house and help him.

The choir moved on to "Hark! The Herald Angels Sing," but I kept trying to figure out the last two lines of "Good King Wenceslas."

Therefore Christian men be sure,
wealth or rank possessing,

Ye who now will bless the poor,
shall yourselves find blessing.

———

"Tonight's blessing was written by Julian of Norwich, a woman who lived in England in the 1300s," said my mother as she opened the mealtime prayers book. "Julian of Norwich was an anchoress. This does not mean that she made anchors for ships. It means that she lived completely alone, to make space for God in her life. She prayed and meditated all day and lived by herself in a little room called a cell that was like a little island attached to a church."

My father took my hand, and I took my mother's hand, who took Davis's hand, who took our father's other hand.

And all shall be well,
and all shall be well,
and all manner of things shall be well.

"Amen," said my mother.
"Amen," said my father, Davis, and I. Then we

had an ordinary supper, if at our house such a thing is possible.

———

"Don't you think that Mrs. Whitmore will say that you have to have a girl Superhero?" Davis and I were working on our homework up in our room. Mrs. Whitmore had been my teacher when I was in third grade. It's a fact: whatever you did, she was always big on having a girl if you had all boys, and on having a boy if you had all girls.

"I have a girl Superhero," said Davis. "Cat Girl."

"You mean Cat Girl who fights Batman and Robin and wears a slinky black costume and a black mask?"

"No," answered Davis. "You're thinking of Cat Woman. I have my own Cat Girl."

He handed me a picture of a regular looking girl with long legs, long, blond hair, and gold wire-rimmed glasses, a girl who looked a little like Leda Johnson. Next to her were three cats.

"What special powers does your Cat Girl have?" I asked.

"Well, she has three cats that she fights criminals with. This first one, Scratchy Cat, has claws painted with Titanium fingernail polish to make them super strong. This one, Stinky Cat, has been specially trained to never give itself a bath. When he shows up he smells up the place so bad that the bad guys beg to go to jail."

"And what's this third one with a big body and a little head?"

"That's Fat Cat. He sits on the crooks until the Police come, and he's so heavy they can't move. Actually, his head is regular size. It just looks small because he's so fat."

———

Like most nights, Davis fell asleep before me. Like most nights, I looked out the window as I lay in bed. The bare trees and the moon shining down on the icy street down below, brought back the words of the song as I slowly drifted off:

> *Good King Wenceslas looked out*
> *on the feast of Stephen.*

When the snow lay round about,
deep and crisp and even.
Brightly shone the moon that night,
though the frost was cruel . . .

Deep in the night I had a dream. In my dream there was a boy about my own age, about my own size. I couldn't see the boy's face because he was bending over a long, long table full of shoes all in a jumbled pile—as though he was searching for something.

The shoes were all dirty and worn, and they gave off a dusty smell, an old smell. In the dream, I called out to the boy again and again, asking him what he was looking for. And still the boy kept on looking and looking—as though he was hoping to find something.

Something extraordinary.

8

Seeing a Pattern

As far as I could tell, Wednesday and Thursday were just ordinary days. Nothing particularly special happened—still no mystical experience.

Nothing at school. Nothing at home. Nothing on the way home.

Nothing.

So on Thursday after school, I decided to go to the library again and took two more pages of notes—just in case.

———

On Friday for morning reflections Mr. Phillips

talked about the invisible. He told the class that he wanted us to start looking for "visible signs of the invisible." I was not exactly sure what that meant. Mr. Phillips said that love, for example, was invisible but that there were visible signs of it, the same for lots of other things, like hate, or jealousy, or hope.

He said that special people all through history had talked about an invisible golden thread that connected people to other people and connected events to other events. A thread that tied our time to the past and to the future. He said these people who could see invisible connections were called mystics. Mr. Phillips finished morning reflections by passing out white drawing paper and telling everyone that we needed to take out a pencil not a pen.

"Today for art class, I want you to keep thinking about the invisible patterns that not only mystics but also artists help us to see." Art was not a normal part of the school day in Mr. Phillips' class. On average we had art about once a week.

"Today I am going to ask each of you to become an artist and help to show us something that we didn't really see before by making what is called a rubbing.

142

To demonstrate this I need to borrow someone's shoe." Mr. Phillips began walking up and down the rows looking at each person's feet.

"Ah, Leda, I see that you have worn your purple hiking boots today. I wonder if I could borrow one of them for a moment." Leda took off one of her purple boots and handed it to Mr. Phillips. I noticed that she had bright orange socks on underneath.

To Nitro, I used to call Leda's purple hikers her Barney Boots. I know that just because I never said this when she could hear it didn't exactly make me a candidate for Nicest Boy in Class, or even Funniest Boy. But you've got to remember that this was before I got to know Leda.

"Now I need two more people to help. David, would you come up and hold Leda's boot nice and steady with the sole facing us so that everyone can see it. And Theresa, would you hold my piece of drawing paper somewhat tightly on the sole so that it won't slip."

David and Theresa took their positions alongside Mr. Phillips in front of the class.

"Now watch what happens. As I rub the side of

my pencil on the paper, invisible patterns begin to come out. The one thing that you have to do is try to stop near the edge of the thing you are rubbing." As Mr. Phillips rubbed his pencil on the paper, a pattern began to appear—one that looked like the bottom of Leda's boot, but at the same time was also slightly different from it, if that makes any sense.

"Right away we should begin to see things that we didn't see before. One reason we didn't see these things is because we weren't looking for them. And that is one of the jobs of the artist—*to move us from inattention to attention.*

"The second reason we didn't see these things before is because the rubbing changes them a little. And that is a second job of the artist—*to make familiar things that we see every day look a little different, a little unfamiliar, a little strange.*"

Mr. Phillips finished his rubbing and held it up high to show the class. "Thank you, David and Theresa. You may sit down. And Leda, thank you for your contribution." He handed Leda her purple hiking boot, and she put it back on.

"Your assignment for art today is to do a rubbing of something that reveals a pattern. Now let me warn you, some things will make good rubbings and some things won't. You will have to experiment. I have lots of paper, so don't worry if your first choice isn't particularly interesting. If your first rubbing doesn't work, try another. And another. Keep making rubbings until you find a pattern that makes us look. Keep trying until you have one that makes us see something that we didn't see before.

"After you have a rubbing that you like, you have one more assignment. You must put some words with your art. Adding words makes your creation an 'inter-disciplinary' piece, and these are very big now days. Some of you may have noticed the inter-disciplinary piece that I have up on the bulletin board by my desk—my picture of the Oxford Cleric with the lines from *The Canterbury Tales*. The words you add can be a paragraph or a sentence, or they can be just words or even just one word. The choice is yours.

"Finally, I have one more piece of paper that I would like to show you."

"This," Mr. Phillips took the top notice from under the extra-big push pin on his bulletin board, "is a memo from the headmaster. It says that since lots of parents will be coming to the Christmas concert tonight, it would behoove us to have work from the students in each class on display in the halls. *Behoove* is a fancy word that means that St. Luke's is big on displaying student work when parents come. So whatever you make this morning will get put up outside class for your parents to see tonight so that they can be extremely proud of you.

"Here are the rubbing rules: 1) You may go anywhere on school or church grounds that you are normally allowed to go; 2) You may not do a rubbing that someone else does; 3) You may not disturb any class. If you do, then you will be made into a rubbing. That makes no sense, but you get the point. And 4) You must be back in class and finished when the next bell rings. Any questions? Then ready . . . set . . . go!"

In spite of Mr. Phillips' racing start, the class was slow to begin getting up and moving around with our paper and pencils. Like Mr. Phillips had said, not everything made a good rubbing. For example, a face did not make a good rubbing, especially your own face. Soon students were asking for more paper.

I sat at my desk and thought and rubbed my eyebrows and then tried to do a rubbing of my eyebrows, which didn't work, and then I thought some more. Finally I got up and went to the front and asked Mr. Phillips for some new sheets of paper. Then I went to the cloakroom in the back and got my hat, coat, and gloves.

Taking my sheets of paper and my pencil, I went outside.

———

Every St. Luke's student knew that we were allowed to go into the old graveyard next to the church, but we had to behave respectfully and were never allowed to play there. Mr. Phillips always called it the churchyard. No matter what you called it, it was still full of graves.

Like most students, I had been inside the old wrought-iron fence that surrounded the cemetery a couple times, but not for very long. I would never admit it, but it was a creepy place, even in daytime, particularly if you were by yourself. I had looked at the graves many times from outside the fence.

Now I had an idea.

I walked past Mr. Phillips' car at the end of the parking lot and stopped at the cemetery gate. A blanket of dry, powdery snow had smoothed over the burial ground's bumps and ridges, and a soft wind blew the top layer like dust over the level whiteness. Above me the low clouds were heavy and gray. The graveyard was bordered by big oaks, the kind that kept their dry, brown leaves all winter. As the wind moved among the branches, the leaves made a soft rasping "Sssssss…" that blended with the soft hiss of the blowing snow.

I lifted the latch on the rusty gate. And then with a big, creaky squeak like you hear in scary movies just before something bad happens, I went in.

Walking carefully to avoid stepping on the graves, I looked through the tombstones. Some were new, some were old. Some were really old. I hunted through row after row and finally found one that seemed unusual.

By carefully rubbing one sheet at a time, each on a different section, I was able to get the entire tombstone on four sheets of paper. When I was finished rubbing all the pages, this is what it said:

ROBERT HAYDEN 1756-1776

I have but one request to make at my departure from this world: It is the charity of its silence. Let no man write my epitaph.

For as no man who knows my motives dare now speak up to vindicate them, so neither let prejudice or ignorance criticize them. Let them rest in obscurity and peace. Let my memory be left in oblivion and my tomb remain uninscribed until other times and other men can do justice to my character.

When my country takes her place among the nations of the earth, then, and not till then, let my epitaph be written.

When I was finished rubbing, I took the four sheets of paper and went back to class. After I taped them together, I had just enough time to add the following words on a fifth sheet taped on below:

Even though he is buried in St. Luke's churchyard, probably no one today knows for sure who Robert Hayden was or how he died. But we do know that he was only twenty years old and that he died in the first year of the Revolutionary War. So maybe he died fighting against the English. Maybe his friends and family did not understand why he fought or why he had to be different. Maybe they thought he was a traitor but really maybe he was a hero. Now we can put ourselves in his shoes and see what he fought for—a new nation that was to come.

I turned in my project just as the bell rang.

———

At seven that night, I came back to St. Luke's with my parents and Davis for the Christmas concert. After thinking about it for a long time, I had finally decided what I wanted to bring for Boxing Day.

I hadn't said anything to my parents but had stopped by myself at the sports store on the way home from school and had bought a pair of gym shoes with some of the money I had gotten for my birthday. I thought about getting cheap ones, but in the end, I got a nice pair, the kind I would have liked to have myself.

As I got into the car to go to the concert with my shoebox in the plastic bag from the sports store, I noticed that Davis had decided to bring a big bag of food, and I smiled.

———

On the way to the chapel where the concert would be, we walked past the classrooms. Each one had student projects displayed on the walls outside. I saw my rubbing about Robert Hayden. Next to it was Nitro's picture. He had made a rubbing of several of the little interconnected pentagons on a soccer ball with the words "Strength Through Unity!" on it. Nearby was a rubbing of a cat's paw that Leda had made even though there were no cats at St. Luke's, at least none that I knew of. Below her picture, Leda had written:

Macavity's a Mystery Cat:
    he's called the Hidden Paw —
For he's the master criminal
    who can defy the Law.
He's the bafflement of Scotland Yard,
    the Flying Squad's despair:
For when they reach the scene of the crime
    — Macavity's not there!

I wondered where Leda had found a cat. I wondered even more how she got it to hold still so she could make a rubbing of its paw. I couldn't decide if Leda's rubbing was more cool or more bizarre. There was a gold star on top of Nitro's, Leda's, mine, and a few others. This was Mr. Phillips' highest grade for art projects.

Down the hall, I could hear *oohs*, *ahs*, and laughter coming from a large crowd that was gathered around "A Gallery of Superheroes by Davis Farrel."

"Very fine work, boys," said my father.

"Yes, we are extremely proud of both of you," my mother added.

"Hello, everyone, and welcome to our annual Christmas concert," said Pastor Jill. For the special evening, she had worn a fancy red velvet dress, and in it she looked, well, extraordinarily extraordinary.

"I want to begin by thanking all of you for coming out on such a chilly evening. We are very glad that you could make it. I know that our students have been practicing hard for this.

"I also want to thank all of you for the gifts you have donated for Boxing Day. Boxing Day comes from a very old English tradition. Each year on the 26th of December, the parish priest would unlock the Poor Box in the back of the church and would use the money to help the needy in the community. By the number of donations that I can see under the tree," Pastor Jill stood on her tiptoes, shaded her eyes with her hand, and looked over toward the pile of presents, "I know that you will be making a lot of people feel very remembered. So again, thank you.

"For our opening prayer tonight I would like to

use one of the verses from 'O Come, O Come, Emmanuel,' a song you will hear later on in the evening. This verse asks that all our differences might be set aside, particularly at this special time of the year:

> *O come, Desire of Nations, bind*
> > *in one the hearts of all mankind.*
> *Bid thou our sad divisions cease,*
> > *and be thyself our King of Peace.*

"Amen," said Pastor Jill.
"Amen," said everyone.

For a small school, St. Luke's had a lot of different class and choir groups on the program. And so all the Christmas favorites were sung, including the one about the twelve days of Christmas, which was performed by Davis's class with Mrs. Whitmore directing. The class was divided into groups of four. Davis's group did "eight maids a-milking" and "three French hens" each time it came around. The song concluded with a big, long, loud "and a par-tri-idge in a pear tree!"

Everyone gave them a long, loud round of applause.

Mrs. Whitmore smiled and bowed and waved to the third graders to take a bow. Her smile was the kind that said 1) she appreciated the applause for her students, and 2) she was glad it was over and no one had messed up on the numbers or come in on the wrong day.

After the third graders sang, the Concert Choir went up and performed the selections we had been practicing for the past two months. Then the program went back to songs by each grade in order, starting with the fourth graders. This way the Concert Choir members, who were mostly in the upper grades, got a chance to rest before they performed again with their classes.

When it came time for the sixth graders to sing, we did the song our grade always did: "I Wonder As I Wander." But this year was different, because in addition to Mrs. Jubal on the piano accompanying us, Theresa Anwar played the violin. We ended with just the voices on the slow, sad last line, "I wonder as I wan-*der* out under the sky," and we really held out the "*der*."

Then just as everyone in the audience thought this was a nice ending and we were done, Theresa came back in with just the violin playing the last line again.

She wore a long, black dress that made her look a lot more, well, a lot more musical than navy or khaki pants and a shirt with a collar and no writing ever did. Without getting all gushy, let me just say that when she held out the high note even longer and sweeter and sadder than our voices had, I thought it was one of the most beautiful things I had ever heard.

And if you think about it, that is something.

Each year most people seemed to like "O Holy Night" the best, especially the parents. Because it was kind of a hard song, it was always sung by the seventh graders. But the song I always liked most was "The Carol of the Bells," which, in my opinion, was even harder. It was always sung by the eighth graders, and each year it was always the very last thing in the program, right after Pastor Jill's Christmas reflections.

———

"Everyone knows who Santa Claus is, especially at this time of year," said Pastor Jill as she began her talk for the evening. "But I wonder if everyone knows who St. Nicholas was and why we call him a saint.

"We might start by asking ourselves, 'What is a saint?' The dictionary has several definitions. Some people think of a saint as a sort of superhero of goodness. But I like to think of a saint as a normal person who does something special, or as an ordinary person who sees the world in an extraordinary way.

"St. Nicholas lived in the fourth century and was the bishop of the church in the city of Myra, in what is now Turkey. Legend and history are intertwined in the story of St. Nicholas's life. The most famous story told about St. Nicholas has to do with three young sisters who lived in his parish. The girls' parents were so poor that they did not have enough money for the daughters to get married. Back then every young girl needed money to pay for her wedding and to set up housekeeping for themselves and their husbands.

"Bishop Nicholas heard about this family and wanted to do something, but he didn't want anyone to know that he was the one helping them. 'How can I give the girls the money they need to get married without the family finding out who gave it?' he asked himself.

"Bishop Nicholas thought and thought, and finally came up with an idea. He climbed up on their roof three nights in a row, and each night he threw a gold coin down their chimney in such a way that it would land in one of the girls' stockings, which were washed and hung each night by the fire to dry.

"After two of the daughters had been able to marry because of the money mysteriously appearing, the father was determined to find out who was helping them. So on the third night, he hid behind the chimney. Along came Bishop Nicholas with his bag of golden coins. When the father heard the footsteps on the roof, he popped out from his hiding place and saw who it was.

"When he was discovered, St. Nicholas asked the father not to tell anyone, but the man wanted the whole city to know what a kind and generous person their bishop was, so he told the story to everyone he knew. Years later, the story goes, after the good bishop died, God rewarded St. Nicholas for his compassion by giving him permission to walk the streets each December on the eve of his feast, bringing gifts to all good children.

"And that is how we came to have the line from the poem which says:

The stockings were hung by the
    chimney with care,
In hope that Saint Nicholas
    soon would be there.

"On behalf of the St. Luke's family, I would like to wish each of you a Christmas full of the kind of love that St. Nicholas showed." Pastor Jill paused a moment to let everyone think about what this really would mean.

"Our final selection this evening will be 'The Carol of the Bells,' and as always it will be performed by the eighth graders together with Twenty-and-One, our handbell choir."

Hark how the bells, sweet silver bells,
    all seem to say, "Throw cares away."

Christmas is here, bringing good cheer,
    to young and old, meek and the bold.
One seems to hear words of good cheer
    from everywhere filling the air.
Merry, merry, merry, merry Christmas!
    Merry, merry, merry, merry Christmas!
On, on they send, on without end,
    their joyful tone to every home.
Dong, ding, dong, ding, dong . . . BONG!

Every year when the eighth graders sang that last BONG! I felt it all the way down to the bottom of my feet. I knew it was coming, but after the long pause when all of a sudden out of the silence they went BONG! it went through me like, well, like I don't know what.

Why did that last BONG! always get to me like that?

I have no earthly idea.

9

No Man Is
an Island

The next day was Saturday. Our reports were due in two days, on Monday, and I was starting to get nervous. The instruction sheet that Mr. Phillips had given us said that our reports needed to be three to five pages long. I figured I could write that much from my notes if I needed to.

But it wouldn't be the same.

Something needed to happen for my mystical experience. But it seemed like the more I tried to make something happen, the less happened. So on Saturday, rather than trying to do something for my report, I stuck to the plans I had.

On the Saturday before Christmas vacation, Mrs. Whitmore's third grade class always went to see the lighting of the huge Christmas tree in Boston. First, there was a sing-along of holiday music that concluded with a lively rendition of "Santa Claus Is Coming to Town" led by the Boston mayor. Then Santa arrived on top of a big red fire truck and flipped a switch that turned on all the lights while everyone clapped and cheered. The ceremony finished up with "We Wish You a Merry Christmas," and then everybody went home.

Afterwards the school trip always went to a restaurant in Deerfield that had a big buffet and Western-style tables, Western-style chairs, and even Western-style pictures in its dining room. The Western stuff was their way to say they had good steaks. Stopping at the buffet for supper was Mrs. Whitmore's way to say she needed parent chaperones.

I had gone with my class when I was in third grade. Mr. Phillips said that Mrs. Whitmore's third graders had been going to see the lighting of the

Boston Christmas tree since 1720.

This had been one of his jokes.

This year Davis was going and so were our parents. They had been the parent chaperons when I went and so to keep everything even, they were going to chaperon Davis's trip.

Our parents were big on having everything even.

St. Luke's was big on having parent chaperons.

The trip didn't leave until after lunch, so on Saturday morning we had our normal piano and swimming lessons. Nitro's sister, Hannah Louise, was going on the trip too, so I had been invited to spend the afternoon and part of the evening over at Nitro's. The third graders and their chaperons would be returning to Winston around eight-thirty. I was supposed to have supper with the Epsteins and to be home when my parents and Davis got back.

———

The snow on Wolman Hill sparkled in the late afternoon sun and was just right for sledding. Not too dry, not too wet. From the top, Nitro and I could see the town of Winston spread out all around us like one of those little villages that people put up with their electric train sets each December. Pulling Nitro's two-man toboggan, we hiked up and slid down more times than we counted, together with little kids, big kids, and adults with sleds, saucers, inner tubes, and cardboard boxes.

We went down with Nitro first and then with me first. With one of us facing forward and one backwards. With me lying on top of Nitro, and with Nitro lying on top of me. With one standing and one sitting. We even went down with both of us standing.

At least part of the way.

Around four o'clock, the sun started to go down and people began to go home. Because the Epsteins always ate late on Saturday nights, we still had a couple of hours before supper. We decided to drop off Nitro's toboggan and get his soccer ball, and then walk back to the Winston hockey rink which had been shoveled out on the river ice. When no one was playing hockey there, we liked kicking the soccer ball on the ice because they left the goalie nets up all winter.

The Avon River flowed right through the middle of town. Like Winston itself, the river was pretty small. Once during Question Time, Leda had asked why the town of Winston had named its river after a cosmetic company. Mr. Phillips did not laugh at her question. He told her that the river in Winston and the make-up were both named after a river in England. Then Nitro had raised his hand and asked what the name of the river in England was. Then Mr. Phillips did laugh and asked Nitro if this was supposed to be a rhetorical question.

Winston's park, the place where I always walked Cathode, was next to the town square, and the Avon River was on the other side of the park. A long time ago, the city council had a small dam, or spillway, built where the river flowed out of the downtown. The dam was only about four feet tall, but it made the river back up and widen out behind it into sort of a long, skinny lake.

In the summer, the park along the river was always full of softball players, picnickers, walkers, and joggers, and people who just sat on the benches. In the winter there were sledders, walkers, joggers, and cross country skiers, but once the sun went down and it got colder, the park was almost always empty.

The town of Winston was extraordinarily careful about almost everything, but the thing that Winston was the most careful about was the ice on the Avon River. No one could go on the ice until the chief of the fire department said that it was thick enough.

And that meant no one.

There was a big flagpole in the park. In the summer they flew the American flag from it. But as soon as the river froze over, they took down the American flag and hung up a big red one that said DANGER! STAY OFF THE ICE! Then when it was cold enough for the chief to drive his fire department car on the river, they took the red flag down and put up a big green one that said THE ICE IS SAFE! In the spring when things started to melt, they put the red flag back up.

———

Nitro spoke loudly in his announcer voice: "The clock is ticking down . . . St. Luke's has one last chance to win . . . Epstein has the ball and a chance

166

to be the hero . . . He gets past one Winston player . . . past another . . . There's nothing between him and the net now but the Winston Elementary goalie . . . Five, four, three, two, one, BAM!" Nitro kicked the ball as hard as he could toward the ice hockey net where I was supposed to be a Winston Elementary goalie crouching to defend it.

As Nitro kicked, he also slipped. Up the ball sailed, passing high over my head and into the darkness.

"Yes, another sad day for St. Luke's." Now I spoke loudly in my own announcer voice. "Epstein seems to have forgotten he was playing soccer and has kicked a field goal instead—giving Winston Elementary the championship again for the billionth time."

"Very funny," said Nitro as he got up and brushed himself off. "Let's go find the ball." In the winter, Nitro refused to wear a hat. He said that his thick brown hair was like a hat. Sometimes when it was really cold and if he were doing something that made him breathe hard, the water vapor would freeze on his hair, making him look like an ice man or some-

167

thing.

With only the lights from the park to shine on this part of the frozen river, it wasn't easy to tell what was a soccer ball and what was a ball-sized chunk of icy snow. As we hunted for the ball, the faint lights sparkled in the ice crystals in Nitro's hair-hat.

After a few minutes of looking together, we split up. The quiet was broken only by the crunch, crunch, crunch of our boots and an occasional "Ouch!" or "Rats!" when one of us kicked what we thought was the ball, only to have it be something frozen very solid. Down the river we could hear the soft rush from where the water poured out from under the ice and over the spillway.

After a few minutes I heard Nitro call out, "Hey, Todd! Over here!"

I followed the sound of Nitro's voice across the river to the far bank.

"Can you believe it?" he asked. While all of the rest of the river was frozen rock-hard with a thick layer of ice on top, the soccer ball had landed right in the middle of a small circle of open water near the bank where a drainage pipe was dripping.

"How are we going to get it now?" asked Nitro. The little circle of water was only about ten or twelve feet across, but there was no way to reach the ball bobbing gently out in the middle.

I looked around for a branch, but the nearest trees were back in the park on the other side of the river. Downstream, about fifty yards away, was the spillway. On our side of the river there was only a broad meadow with the brown tops of dead grass and weeds sticking out above the snow.

I got an idea. "Hit it with snow and knock it over to the side so we can grab it."

For about five minutes, Nitro and I pelted the ball with snowballs and chunks of ice, until it was almost to the edge where we could reach it. We could have gotten it over to the side of the hole sooner, but Nitro started us both laughing by doing a scene from a movie that we had watched together, and we couldn't throw straight.

"I'm sorry, Wilson!" yelled Nitro. Splash went his snowball. "Please forgive me, Wilson!" Splash, another miss. "Come back, Wilson!"

In spite of Nitro making us laugh, there were

enough hits to gradually move the soccer ball closer. Even when we missed, the waves we made helped to float it over to the side. Finally, it was about three feet from the edge, but the current of the river running below the ice created a little eddy that kept it there, just out of reach.

"Hold my arm so I can lean out and try to get it with my foot," said Nitro.

I grabbed Nitro's arm and leaned back. Nitro stood at the edge and reached out as far as he could with his leg. With his toe he could just touch the ball but couldn't bring it closer.

"I . . . can't . . . get . . . it," said Nitro as he leaned with all his might.

"Kick it!" I said. "Kick it really hard so it will go up on the ice."

Nitro pulled his foot back and BAM! gave the ball a mighty kick so that it shot completely out of the hole and sailed down the frozen Avon into the dark night.

Suddenly, without any warning, the ice beneath Nitro collapsed.

As the ice broke and Nitro went into the water,

I slipped and fell backwards onto the frozen river, losing my grip on Nitro's arm. I watched helplessly as for a split second he tried to grab at the broken ice pieces. As he struggled in the freezing-cold water, he looked up and gave me a quick desperate look. Our eyes met.

Then, caught in the current, Nitro disappeared below the surface.

"Nitro!" I screamed, and spreading flat on the ice to distribute my weight, like I had seen on TV, I scrambled back to the weakened edge.

A second or two ticked by as I peered into the swirling surface. Nothing!

"Nitro!" I yelled again down at the water.

Again nothing.

Suddenly an idea came to me, and I plunged my arm deep into the icy water trying to find something I could grab.

"Take my hand, Nitro!" I shouted. "TAKE MY HAND!"

Another second or two. Still nothing.

Even with only my arm in the water, I knew Nitro was in danger. Almost instantly my fingers and hand had gone numb and stiff. Worse yet, below the dark surface I could feel the current flowing much stronger than it seemed to from above.

I knew Nitro would have trouble coming back up where the hole was.

"Nitro! The current's taking you!" I shouted as loudly as I could towards the open water. "COME TO MY VOICE! Come upriver!"

A few more seconds ticked by. Again and again I swished with my numb hand and arm, my movements made even clumsier by my water-soaked jacket sleeve and thick gloves. I couldn't see a thing below the surface.

Except for the splashing I made, the night was eerily calm and silent. The only other sound was the rush of water from the spillway downstream and my own breath, now coming in gasps.

What to do? I looked around wildly for help and saw no one. *What to do?*

"Nitro! Nitro!" I yelled again down at the open water. "Swim to the hole!"

Another second of silence. Another.

Then in desperation, I got another idea. I stuck

172

my whole head underneath the water and yelled.

"NII-TROO!"

My voice drifted off into the depths making the odd sound that voices make underwater, distant and dream-like.

The shock of the cold took my breath away, and I raised my head sputtering for air. With my hair dripping freezing-cold water, I took three quick breaths and plunged my head under again.

"NIII-TROOO!" I yelled once more, and this time I thought to open my eyes like I did when I swam at the pool. In the dark I could just barely see Nitro. He was at the water's surface a few yards downstream, trying to get a breath in a small pocket of air under the ice.

I jumped to my feet and ran to the spot where I thought Nitro would be. Dropping to the snow, I scraped furiously to clear an open spot.

"Nitro! I'm here!" I yelled as I scraped. "I'm here! Hold on!"

Suddenly a patch of clear ice appeared through the snow, and below it I could see Nitro. Fighting the current, he was holding on to the end of a tree branch that stuck down from the frozen surface. He was pressing his face and mouth up into an open space of one or two inches of air between the water and ice. Frantically I clawed away the snow to make the clear spot bigger.

"I'm here! I'm here, Nitro!" I yelled, putting my mouth down close. When he didn't seem to hear me, I slapped the ice with my frozen hands to make a noise. At the sound, Nitro looked up. His face was already stark white, his lips purple-blue. It had been barely thirty seconds since he had fallen in.

"Swim! Swim hard, Nitro! GET BACK TO THE HOLE!" I shouted. As I yelled, I frantically pointed back to where the hole in the ice was, maybe three yards upstream.

Our eyes met again and locked. Nitro was only inches away but in a different world. His face showed panic and exhaustion. Through the ice, I saw Nitro shake his head as he mouthed the words, "I can't."

"Yes, you can! You CAN!" I beat on the ice with my fists. Tears began to stream from my eyes. "You can do it, Nitro! You can swim back! You can! You're a fighter! You're strong! Don't you give up!

Nitro! You swim back to the hole! You do it now! YOU SWIM BACK THERE NOW!"

Below in the watery depths Nitro made no response as he struggled to get breaths while the waves from the flowing river made the air pocket now a little bigger, now a little smaller.

In my heart, I knew that Nitro could never swim back upstream. Maybe in the summer, when the water was warm, maybe when he was not wearing heavy clothing. But not now, not tonight. But what to do? What to do?

"All right! Stay there! STAY THERE, NITRO!" I yelled. "I'll break through!"

Nitro appeared to hear me or at least to understand because he gave a weak nod. I looked around for something to use on the ice, but there was nothing but shadowy, gray whiteness as far as I could see. In frustration I tried jumping up and down as hard as I could to try to make a crack. But the river ice was solid.

I knew that even if I could find a rock, even if I had a hammer, Nitro could not hold out long enough.

Desperately, I looked around for help. I scanned both shorelines in vain. Then I looked downriver fifty yards to the spillway and dropped down once more to the ice.

"Nitro, look at me! LOOK AT ME! You have to swim for the spillway! THE SPILLWAY!" I shouted as I pointed downriver. "Swim to the spillway, and I will find you! You hear me? I WILL FIND YOU!"

Nitro looked up. He didn't or couldn't shout back, but his eyes showed that he had understood. I put my lips to the ice one more time. "SWIM TO THE SPILLWAY NOW!" I shouted. "I WILL FIND YOU!"

Nitro gave me one last look and then a quick nod. Through my tears I nodded back. I watched as he took one last deep breath, let go of the branch, and floated out of view.

I was paralyzed for a moment, staring at the empty spot where he had been.

Then I started running as hard as I could towards the spillway.

After yelling and digging and jumping, after being wet and freezing—running in the snow was not easy. Pain shot through my lungs and my breath came in frantic gulps, in-out, in-out, as I scrambled the fifty yards that never seemed to end. As I ran, something in my mind grabbed on to the words and said them over and over: *I will find you I will find you I will find you.*

But I didn't know if I was saying this for Nitro or to convince myself.

Now the spillway was just ten yards away, but I felt like I couldn't take another step. As my legs started to slow, in my mind I heard Nitro's voice saying, *Find your power! Find your power!* and I kept on running.

It had been maybe a minute and a half since he first fell in.

Suddenly, either because the current was swifter near the dam or because all my tiredness and the uneven snow had really cost me time, I saw Nitro shoot out over the spillway ahead of me!

In that instant the world slowed.

Suddenly there was no thinking, there were no thoughts.

There was no talking, there were no words.

There was only one thing. And in that instant, I crossed the final yards and dove head first over the dam after him.

The spillway was only a little more than four feet tall, but I felt for a second like I was floating on air. Except for the gentle noise of the flowing water, the night was utterly quiet and unreal.

Suddenly, splash! The icy water hit me, and immediately I was back in normal time.

I will find you I will find you I will find you! The words pounded in my head as I was buffeted by the current in the deep pool below the dam. As I was pulled below the surface, I flailed with my hands. Suddenly I felt something soft—Nitro! I hugged him tightly to me with both arms and kicked and kicked and kicked until all at once we both broke the surface and together we gasped for air.

No words now, only air. The icy water made it hard for me to catch my breath. Air, air, air! But now trouble. Trouble! The pool here was deep, deeper than the river. As I held on to Nitro, we went under again, dragged down by the current and our wet clothes.

And Nitro, except for when he had gasped for air at the surface, was not moving at all.

I thought maybe I could touch bottom and then push off to bring us both back up. But there was no bottom. So flutter kick hard, hard, hard. Then finally we broke the surface again and air, air, air, air. Then the sinking again.

Kick, kick, kick, kick—finally air again!

Now time was speeding up. I realized that I would not be able to hold on to Nitro much longer. Saving someone was not like in the movies. Not when you were freezing. Not when you were twelve. Lifeguards made it look easy. It was not easy. Not now, not tonight. Tonight it was not even possible.

Help! I thought as our heads sank below the surface again.

Help us! I said in my thoughts as the icy water flowed over us. *Someone help us. Please help us!*

Now I had to let go of Nitro with one hand so I could swim. And my other hand was so numb and so stiff that I knew I would not have the strength to hold on to him the next time we went under. I flutter kicked, and this time pulled with my free hand to get us back to the surface. Kick, pull, kick, pull—air!

We broke the surface, and we both gasped and coughed. And breathed, and breathed, and breathed. We had drifted downstream, and the water was quieter, but it was still too deep to touch bottom. The shore looked about twenty feet away.

It might as well have been a hundred.

Then slowly we started to sink. I was trying to swim with one arm and to hold on to Nitro with the other, and it was not enough.

Find your power! Find your power! But there was no power left. It was not enough. We were sinking. But I would not let go of Nitro. I had found him. I would *not* let him go.

As my face was about to go under, my mind got very quiet, quieter than it had been since the catastrophe started. And in my mind I said one more time, said quietly this time, *Please . . . someone please help us . . . please.*

Then, just when I thought it was all over, just as we were about to go below the surface again, something bounced against the tip of my nose. Something floating. Something round.

The soccer ball.

I managed to grab it with my free hand and carefully pulled it under me until I was floating on top of it. With my other hand I held Nitro by the coat so his head was above water and he could breathe. Then I kicked for the shore with the little strength I had left.

We moved slowly, but we moved. The current helped. We were about ten feet from the shore. Now five. I was afraid to try standing up because I was afraid the soccer ball would pop out of my numb hand. Now four feet from the shore . . . now three. Finally I tried standing.

I could touch bottom!

Still holding the soccer ball in one hand and dragging Nitro with the other, I waded in to shore and pulled Nitro halfway out. Then I collapsed on the snowy bank.

I had to lie still and count to ten before I had the strength to stand up and drag Nitro all the way out of the water. Then I collapsed again next to him on the snow.

Nitro was breathing and coughing, but his eyes

were closed and his head was bleeding a little where there was a rock-sized bruise. He was as white as the snow he was lying on, and he was shivering so hard that I was afraid he would shake himself to pieces. Through my own shivering lips, I called to Nitro again and again as I knelt beside him.

I begged him to talk to me. I begged him to wake up. He was breathing, but it was clear that Nitro was not going to answer.

It was up to me.

I looked around. We were downstream, not far from the spillway. Next to us on the riverbank was a little jogging trail. Across the jogging trail was the picnic area, then the playground, then the street. Across the street I could see the lights in the windows of St. Joseph's, the Catholic Church. Not that far—maybe two blocks.

I noticed that I was getting clumsy. My shaking and my numbness made it hard to stand up or do anything. My mind was getting numb, too. I looked down and noticed I was still gripping the soccer ball in one arm. Carefully I set it down in the snow, pushing it in so it would not roll away.

Then I tried to pull Nitro to his feet. Surely if I helped him, we could walk the two blocks through the picnic grounds to St. Joe's. Surely.

Except for coughing and shivering, Nitro did not respond. And I realized that there would be no walking him there.

Next, I tried to pick up Nitro in my arms the way the hero in the movie carries his wounded buddy back to safety. One step like this, and I fell forward into the snow with Nitro in front of me. Then I tried to put him across my back like firemen do. We fell forward again, and this time I got the wind knocked out of me by Nitro's weight, and I had to just lie on the snow and breathe for a while.

Carrying someone was not like in the movies.

Finally I just grasped Nitro's hands and started walking backwards, pulling him on his back. It was slow, and it was hard work. But the snow had a smooth icy crust on it, and we made progress. It helped that he was smaller than I was. Every so often my hands would slip, and I would fall backward. Again and again I got back up and dragged Nitro a few more feet.

We were past the jogging trail and in the picnic grounds.

Occasionally off in the distance I could hear a car going by in the street between the park and the church. The first few times this happened, I dropped Nitro's arms, turned around, and tried to yell and wave. Once I even tried to climb up on a picnic table. But my yell was little more than a whimper, and my waving was useless. By the time I turned around, the cars were almost past us anyway, and in the dark we would never be seen.

Besides I was starting to get dizzy, and I kept on getting colder and colder.

So after a couple times, I just ignored the few cars there were and tried to focus on getting Nitro to the church.

Drag, drag, drag, slip. Lie still for just a moment. Catch your breath. Now get back up. Steady, steady. A few more feet. Drag, drag, drag, drag, slip again.

Now we were at the start of the playground, maybe halfway to the church, just a block or so from the street.

But walking backwards on the slippery uneven

ground and dragging Nitro was hard. I was falling more and more. And each time I fell, it took longer to get back up. And each time I got up, I was more exhausted and more dizzy. And I had to wait until the world quit spinning before I could reach down and take Nitro's arms and start again.

And each time, Nitro looked worse.

Finally past the slides . . . Finally past the swings . . . Finally past the benches . . . I tried to think how long it had been since Nitro had first fallen through the ice. I guessed it had been maybe six or seven minutes, but my mind was not working very well.

Now we were through the playground, perhaps ten yards to get to the street and then across it to St. Joe's.

Ten little yards and then the street.

Boom! I slipped once more and fell backwards. This time hard. This time because the ground behind me had begun to rise up a little just before the street. Not a real hill, not something that would have even made me out of breath if I had run up it in the summer. Now it seemed like a mountain.

I took three deep breaths, took Nitro's hands in

185

mine, and started up. We got about five steps when suddenly I lost my footing again, and Nitro and I slid back down to the bottom in a jumbled heap. I struggled up but fell right back down. And this time as I lay on my back and looked up at the whirling sky, I was so dizzy I almost blacked out.

Sire the night is darker now,

and the wind blows stronger . . .

I suddenly realized for the first time that there was a chance we might not make it.

Fails my heart, I know not how,

I can go no longer . . .

I lay on my back in the snow for a full thirty seconds and waited for the spinning to stop, but this time it wouldn't stop. What to do?

I thought that maybe I could leave Nitro here and go on alone for help. What if I blacked out before I could tell them where he was?

No. We go together, or not at all. Together. Or not at all.

I looked over at where Nitro lay. My best friend had stopped shivering and now was lying still. Perfectly still. Completely still. So still, as if, as if . . .

186

With my last bit of strength, I forced myself to stagger back up, to grab Nitro's arms, and to start up the incline again. Now my mind was not quiet. It was not slowed down. It was shut down. There was around five yards of uphill climb to reach the edge of the park and the road.

No thinking. No nothing. Just drag, step together. Drag, step together.

Drag . . . step together . . . Drag . . . step together. STOP.

Stop. I simply could not pull anymore. Nitro simply would not come anymore. We were stopped, completely stopped, halfway up the little hill. I could hold us there, but could not go further. This was it.

I felt so alone.

And for the second time that night, tears began to roll from my eyes. I stood and cried, and cried and shivered. My back ached, my legs ached, everything ached. And at the same time everything was cold and numb. Still I would not let go of Nitro's arms. I would not let go.

And then gradually, as the tears dropped from my cheeks down to the snow, from somewhere, somewhere that was not me, words came to my mind, the same words over and over and over.

No man is an island. Each one is part of the main.

No man is an island. Each one is part of the main.

No man—drag—is an island. Each one—step together—is part of the main.

No man—drag—is an island. Each one—step together—is part of the main.

Over and over and over until somehow I was crying, and laughing, and shivering, and standing at the top of the little hill. And there was Nitro, my best friend of all time, with me, lying on the snow at my feet.

Across the street, behind two towering bare oak trees, just a half-block away now, the lights of St. Joseph's glowed through the stained glass windows. I saw Father Martin, one of the priests, come out of the big wooden front door with a broom to brush the snow off the steps before Saturday night Mass.

I opened my mouth to cry out for help, but no cry was there. Only a croak came out, a raspy whisper.

Inside someone had started ringing the big church bell.

DONG-dong. Pause. DONG-dong. The bell said.

"Father Martin, look over here," I said in a tiny voice that I could barely hear myself as the last strength drained out of me.

DONG-dong. Pause. DONG-dong.

"Father, over here. We need you," I whispered as I slumped first to my knees, then all the way down to the snow.

DONG-dong. Pause. DONG-dong.

Father, help us. Look this way. See us. See us here. I thought as my head sank to the ground.

———

DONG-dong.

Down, down, down into the soft, powdery, comfortable snow.

DONG-dong.

Down to a place with no return.

DONG-dong.

Down, down into a darkness lovely and deep.

DONG . . . DONG . . . DONG.

10

It's Been Real

I was warm.

That was good—it was good to be warm. Warm was good. I was not ready to wake up or open my eyes yet, and I let the warmness drift in and out of my mind as I myself drifted in and out.

After some time in this comfortable state, I noticed a second thing.

I had no clothes on.

And that was good, too—or was it? Did people go naked in heaven? Or was that the Garden of Eden or something? Or was that Davis's project? I let these more scattered thoughts go in and out of my mind for some time, as I continued to go in and out myself, although now I was definitely more in than out.

After a shorter time, I noticed a third thing. I was in bed, but it was not my bed. And it was not my parents' bed, or any bed that felt familiar. I was under a warm, cozy electric blanket that clicked on every so often and then later would click off. Click on . . . click off . . . on . . . off . . . But my mother had gotten rid of our electric blankets because of something about magnetic fields.

So where was I?

With this thought I woke up and opened my eyes. The first thing I saw was a young girl dressed in a long white robe. Her back was to me, and her golden hair glowed and shimmered like a halo around her head. Behind her a massive, black leather Bible sat on a graceful wooden stand. Next to the Bible was a shining chalice. And next to the chalice was the soccer ball! The young girl in the white robe was holding a long, golden candlestick with a big white candle on top.

I opened my mouth and tried to speak. "Am I . . . am I . . . in heaven?" I finally managed to say.

The angel with the golden hair turned around and looked at me and smiled. "No, silly. You're in Winston!" The candlelight glinted off her golden wire-rimmed glasses, and all at once I recognized her.

It was Leda.

"But, but . . ." I stammered as I gazed in wonder and confusion at her white robe and golden candlestick.

"But what, Todd?"

"Are you really . . . are you really . . . an angel?"

"No, silly," Leda said for the second time that night and laughed. "I'm an altar girl! And Father Martin is getting ready to say six o'clock Mass, but actually now it's going to be more like six-fifteen Mass, because he had to call Nitro's parents to come and get you. That was after he found you two soaking wet across the street in the snow, and he and my dad had to carry you into the rectory."

"Nitro! How is Nitro?" I blurted out as it all suddenly came rushing back.

"Nitro is fine. He's in the other bedroom, and he's awake and talking his head off as usual. My dad is staying with him until his parents come. I was assigned to stay with you. Speaking of heads, Nitro has a massive bump on the front of his, but my dad says that he's going to be fine."

"But, but . . ." Information was coming at me faster than I could make sense of it.

"But what, Todd? Really, you would think that it was you who had gotten a massive bump on the head and not Nitro."

"But shouldn't Nitro go to the hospital or see a doctor or something?

"My dad *is* a doctor. Don't you know anything about me?"

At that moment another girl dressed in a long white robe and also carrying a golden candlestick appeared at the door.

"Hey, Leda, Father Martin wants to know if Todd is awake and if you think you can leave him alone, or if we should start without you," she said.

"Nitro," I said. "Where's Nitro?"

"I think he's okay," Leda said to the second angel. Then turning back to me she said, "Todd, I would like you to meet Ruby Malone, my best friend. She goes to St. Joe's with me, and we trained to be altar girls together. Ruby, tell Father Martin please not to start without me. Todd seems to have recovered sufficiently, so I'll be right there."

"Got it." Ruby rushed out, and Leda turned back to me.

"Now listen. Listen carefully because you're still acting a bit, well—I hope you take this in the proper spirit—a bit bizarre.

"I have to go help with Mass. My dad, *Doctor Johnson*, checked you and Nitro, and you're both okay. I repeat—*You are both okay*. He says that neither of you was in the water or out in the cold long enough to cause any real problems. He thinks Nitro is going to have one giant headache tomorrow, but says that for two guys who decided to go swimming in December, you're in great shape.

"My dad is waiting down the hall with Nitro until his parents come to pick you both up. Nitro's parents are going to keep an eye on you until your parents get back from the excursion to Boston with Mrs. Whitmore's class. You got all that?"

I just nodded my head.

"You know, you have the drollest smile on your

face," Leda told me. "But it's kind of cute in a way. By the way, Nitro was all worried about his soccer ball, so Father Martin asked me to run out in the snow and find it. I set it up here so you won't forget it. Now I have got to go! I'll see you Monday in school." Leda grabbed her candlestick and rushed out.

A moment later she appeared again.

"Here are your clothes," Leda said tossing a jumbled pile on the chair next to the bed. "You do know that you have no clothes on, don't you? Father Martin and my dad put all your wet stuff in the dryer with Nitro's when you first got here."

Suddenly I realized what Leda was saying, and I gasped and pulled the electric blanket tighter around me.

"Oh, don't get all histrionic," Leda said. "I was in the narthex ringing the bell and didn't see anything. That was around thirty or forty minutes ago, so everything should be adequately dry by now."

And with that Leda was gone again. I was just about to get up when all of a sudden her head stuck back in around the doorway.

195

"And oh, I forgot to tell you," Leda added in a voice that was out of breath, like she had just run back. "The way that you saved Nitro out there tonight—by jumping into the river after him—was stupendous, truly stupendous."

And then Leda disappeared again, and this time she did not return. I closed my eyes and laid my head back on the pillow. I took a few deep breaths, and just let the good news wash over me for a while.

And all shall be well, and all shall be well, and all manner of things shall be well. The words kept going through my mind, and I smiled. Then I added one more thing.

Thank you.

Then I got up and got dressed—which took a little more time than normal because I was still a little overwhelmed by everything. Finally I grabbed the soccer ball and went to find Nitro.

———

Leda had been right. Nitro was okay. As I walked down the hallway to the other bedroom, I could hear his voice going nonstop to Leda's father about something. I stepped through the doorway and stood still. Nitro was already dressed and was sitting on the bed holding an ice pack against a very bad-looking lump on his forehead. Nitro glanced up and saw me in the doorway. He stopped talking.

For a second we were silent.

Then Nitro jumped up, and I dropped the soccer ball, and we rushed together, and we just kept hugging each other.

And then Nitro found his voice, or a part of his voice, and said in words that only I could hear, "See? I knew you could do it!" Then with blurry eyes— his and mine—he added in an even softer voice that cracked as he spoke, "I was . . . I was so scared . . . but you found me."

———

A few minutes later Nitro's parents arrived. They had been on their way home from attending the Jewish synagogue in Deerfield, and it had taken a while to locate them. When they came into the room, there were a lot more hugs for both Nitro and me. And everyone got, well, a little gushy for a while.

Then together Nitro and I told them the story from start to finish. When we were done, Mrs. Epstein gave me yet another big hug, told me thank you a bunch of times, and everyone got kind of choked up again. When she finished, Mr. Epstein did the same, except he shook my hand. Then Mr. and Mrs. Epstein stepped out into the hall to speak with Dr. Johnson while Nitro and I put our coats on.

Leda's father told them several times that we both were fine but said that Nitro was going to have a serious headache. He and Father Martin had given him two aspirin, and he said that Nitro would need to keep taking them every four hours. If that did not help or if he developed any other problems, they were supposed to call him at home.

Then Nitro and I got into the car with his parents. Just as we were about to drive off, the big church door burst open and Leda came running out at full speed, her white robe streaming behind her. In her arms she had the soccer ball.

Without breaking stride, Leda tossed the ball in to Nitro who had rolled down the window. As she raced back up the steps, she yelled back to us over her shoulder, "Don't forget it the next time you lads go for a dip!"

Then with a BOOM! the church door closed behind her, and she was gone.

———

Twenty minutes later we were all sitting together around their dinner table spread with food, and unless you looked at Nitro's head, it almost seemed as though it had been, well, a perfectly ordinary day.

Before we ate, Mrs. Epstein opened up *The Jewish Blessings Book* and set in it front of her. Then she took my hand, and I took Mr. Epstein's hand, who took Nitro's hand, who took his mother's other hand, and she read:

Blessed art Thou, O Lord, our God,
    King of the Universe.
You bring forth good things from the Earth.
And it is by your will that all things
    come to pass.

"Amen," said Mrs. Epstein.

"Amen," said Mr. Epstein, and Nitro, and I.

While everyone ate, Nitro and I went through the story one more time. Nitro said that after he let go of the branch, he held his breath for the longest time and swam as hard as he could. Just when he thought he couldn't hold his breath one more second, he found himself suddenly sailing through the air, going over the spillway. He caught a quick breath just before hitting the water. Then he remembered being pushed down by the current and banging his head on a rock on the bottom. The next thing he knew, Father Martin was carrying him into St. Joe's.

Mrs. Epstein asked him if his head hurt, and he said yes. She looked worried and said he could take two more aspirin before he went to bed.

I looked over at Nitro. The bump was still an ugly purple and did not seem like it was going down.

Was it just two hours ago that I had been struggling to get up that little hill?

Finally I said I should probably be going since my parents were expecting me to be home when they got there. Mrs. Epstein wasn't happy about my going home, and she asked about five times if I was sure that I would be okay waiting by myself or if I wanted someone to wait with me.

When I said five times that I would be okay waiting with Cathode, Mr. Epstein said it was okay if I went home, but he would drive me the five blocks and that I was to call them if there was any problem. Before I left, I got Nitro alone and asked if he was all right. He smiled and said sure and tried to look like it was true. But his smile was not very convincing, and his eyes had a look that made me worry.

———

When my parents and Davis got home, I was on the couch with Cathode. The two of us were lying under the afghan watching *If a Monster Answers— Hang Up!*

"It's us, son," my mother called as they came in. As they started taking off their coats, she smiled over at me and asked, "So, Todd, how was your evening?"

"Well . . ." I sat up and tried to think how I could possibly answer this.

"Well," I said. "It's been real."

———

I told them the whole story. Then everyone — my mother, my father, and Davis — made a huge deal out of it and asked me all sorts of questions.

Then my mother had to call Mrs. Epstein. And then my father had to talk with Mr. Epstein. Mr. Epstein said that they had called their own doctor, and he had told them the same thing Leda's father had, that Nitro's head was going to hurt but otherwise he would be okay and that they should call him if Nitro or I showed any changes. And then I had to talk with Nitro. He sounded a little better, but not really. He just didn't sound like himself.

Everyone, including Hannah Louise who finally got on the phone herself, told me about a billion times that they were extremely proud of me. They made such a fuss that I didn't know what to say.

It's a fact: we were on the phone for a long time.

After we hung up, Davis, who I think was the only one who had not talked on the phone, announced to everyone that he had just had an epiphany. He wouldn't tell what it was. He just said he had to work on something up in our bedroom and then ran upstairs, shut the door, and didn't come down for a while.

———

I was tired after all the excitement and went to bed early, even before *If a Monster Answers—Hang Up!* was over, even before Davis.

Maybe because I went to bed so early, it was still dark when I woke up.

I looked at my watch. It was six in the morning. Now I did not feel tired at all. I felt calm but not sleepy, alert but not anxious.

I felt, well, fine.

I stayed in bed for a while but couldn't get back to sleep. For some reason, I felt a strong impulse to get dressed and go outside.

In the dark of the room I pulled my jeans and a sweatshirt over my pajamas. As I quietly went downstairs, I was aware of the surfaces I could feel through my stocking feet as I crossed the carpeted bedroom, went down the hardwood stairs, and tiptoed across the linoleum kitchen floor and got my hat, coat, scarf, gloves, and boots on. I left a note just in case my parents got up before I got back:

> *Went for a walk. Back soon. Don't worry, I am totally okay. Todd*
>   *P.S. Mom, I have my hat and scarf on.*

Mysteriously, Cathode did not stir as I slipped out the porch door and into the early, early morning. Above me all the stars shone brightly. No cars drove in the silent streets. I was the only one up.

———

Unlike most times when I walked, I just let my footsteps take me where they would. I was fully awake, not dull or drowsy. I did not think about anything in particular, but was content to merely take in all the sights and sounds from the world around me.

Gradually my walking led me back to the park and to the sledding path on Wolman Hill. With hardly any effort, I climbed the snow-covered hillside. At the top, I paused and looked out over the sleeping town. Down below, the city lights twinkled like little stars. I found a flat spot and sat down on the packed snow. Faintly, off in the distance, I could hear the gentle sound of the river as it poured over the spill-way.

And I thought about everything that had happened.

It seemed a long time ago, and it seemed like it had just happened. Everything had taken place so slowly, and yet it had all gone so quickly. When I told my parents about it, they had understood. And still, they didn't really understand. How could they?

How could anyone?

In the east, the sky was turning gray and pink. The woods on the edge of town made a jagged line of black against the gray. A breeze stirred, and the air felt fresh and new. As it blew gently against my face, joy came all over me. I took a deep, deep breath, and slowly let it out. As the light began to spread over the town below me, it seemed like a beginning.

I am here. And here is a good place to be, I thought.

I looked up into the morning sky, and it was vast

and endless.

Then I looked down, and I saw Mr. Anwar, Theresa's father, leaving their house to open the restaurant. Mrs. Anwar was dressed in a bathrobe and slippers and holding their new baby. She yawned and kissed him good-bye at the door. Suddenly I understood that owning a restaurant must be hard work, particularly in a new country, particularly after leaving behind everyone you ever knew. I saw that there must be mornings when Mr. Anwar was tired and did not want to get up. But he still did.

Then I thought about my own father and mother getting up every day to go to work, especially when it was dark and cold, and I wondered if they ever were tired. I decided they probably were sometimes, and I wondered why I had never realized this before.

Across the square I saw Pastor Jill pull into the St. Luke's parking lot, the only car there. A tiny square had been scraped clean on the windshield. She pulled into the same spot as always, down at the end of the parking lot under the big oak tree. I watched her get out, cross over to the entrance, unlock the old church door, and go in. A moment later the lights came on and streamed from the windows onto the snow.

I looked at the sun. A red sliver had risen just above the horizon and cast long shadows behind everything. Then I remembered it was the earth that moved. The sun stayed still. Suddenly it seemed like the earth moved beneath me, and I put out a hand to steady myself. Where I put my hand down it felt warm.

As the world turned, I could feel the darkness falling away. I was riding on a huge ball, turning to face a round fire. I listened, and far away I thought I could hear the crackling, steady roar of the sun like a million blazing furnaces. And everywhere I looked, the world seemed full of goodness.

And this was something I had never noticed before.

Then I heard a quiet, constant crackling around me. Next spring's grass buried beneath the snow was burning, so were the roots of the bare trees, deep below the ground, burning, alive, and growing.

I am burning too, I thought. *I am like a furnace of life.*

I listened more intensely, and deep down I heard, or maybe felt, something like a slow, steady heartbeat, like the endless repetition of day and night or the eternal cycle of the seasons. A sound filled with sadness, but more full of joy. Definitely more joy.

Then off in the distance, I heard again the soft sound of rushing water as it passed over the little dam and flowed on downstream. I remembered the floating soccer ball, bobbing next to us in the icy river. How it had appeared . . . mysteriously . . . right when . . . just before . . .

And then I felt the surge of something wonderful. Something just beyond my reach. Something that Leda might call, well, a gloriousness.

And not just a gloriousness but a love.

One that went on and on forever.

———

I was up on the hill for a little while longer. Then it was time to go. The trip home seemed to take no time at all. When I got in, the whole family was still asleep.

I climbed back into bed as drowsiness began to flow over me.

The last thing I remembered was hearing the distant peal of St. Luke's church bells calling the congregation to the early service.

11

Middle C

I woke later in the morning, and it was good this time to wake up in my own bed.

After a proper breakfast and church, I got out all my notes and several sharp pencils and began writing my report. I took a break for lunch around 1 o'clock. Before going back up to my room, I tried calling Nitro for an update. His mother said that 1) Alex was feeling better, but 2) he still had a bad headache, and so 3) he was lying down.

Not good.

Trying not to be too worried, I went back to my report. After a number of revisions and a bit of eyebrow rubbing, I was ready to type it on the computer.

By suppertime I had finished.

———

Finally it was Monday, the last day of school before Christmas break. That morning, we had the ordinary subjects, if you could call what happened in Mr. Phillips' classroom ordinary. After lunch, Mr. Phillips canceled all classes, and each sixth grader had to stand up and read his or her report aloud in front of the room.

Mr. Phillips had suggested that to show a proper respect for our reports, we might want to dress up a bit—each person in his or her own way. Some of the boys in class wore white shirts, and a few wore suit coats. Some of the girls wore dresses. Leda Johnson wore a tie, and so did Mr. Phillips. After thinking for a while, I had chosen to wear the new shirt and pants that I had worn to my cousin's wedding.

Nitro's report, "Let Freedom Explode: An Argument for the Legalization of Firecrackers," was both funny and serious, and it drew laughs and applause from the class. On one side of his forehead, Nitro had a fancy little Band-Aid with tiny soccer balls on it, and except for that he was his old self again, full of life.

Finally I felt like things were, well, getting back to normal.

As he sat down, we gave each other one of our nods as well as a big smile. And I was glad. Very glad.

When it came my turn, I was not really scared or nervous. My report had ended up being longer than I thought it would be. A lot longer. But overall I was happy about the way it had turned out. It's a fact: I had come a long way from Luxemburg.

In more ways than one.

I walked to the front of the classroom, stood next to Mr. Phillips' desk and read:

MYSTICAL EXPERIENCES
by Todd Farrel

A. Introduction
   A mystical experience is when something or some things happen to you

that cannot be explained. People from
all over the world have had mystical
experiences. Some people see God. Some
hear voices. Sometimes there are dead
people in mystical experiences. Sometimes
if mystical experiences happen with small
everyday things they can be hard to see. But
when things you think are unconnected start
to add up, you may see a pattern.

B. Some Famous Mystical Experiences
    Many famous people in history have had
mystical experiences. Moses heard a voice
coming from a burning bush. A poet named
William Blake saw a tree full of angels. One
book I read said that a mystical experience
helps you see the world in a new way.
    Saint Francis lived in Italy around 1200
A.D. One day he heard a voice that said,
"Go and repair my house, which as you
see is falling into ruin." He gave all that
he had to the poor, even his clothes! He
called the sun, Brother Sun, and the moon,

Sister Moon. Lots of people thought he was bizarre, even his own father.

Another famous person who had a mystical experience was Joan of Arc, who lived in France during the 1400s. When she was thirteen, she began to hear voices that seemed to come from a blaze of light. They told Joan she was supposed to help the king of France. Joan listened to the voices and was able to help drive the English out of France. After many battles, she was captured, tried, and put to death by powerful people in the church who did not like it that Joan heard the voices and they didn't. They also did not like that she was different and dressed in men's clothes when she went to war. They thought she should be like everyone else.

Mystical experiences are not just from the Middle Ages. Thomas Merton was a modern-day monk who lived in a monastery in Kentucky. Monks live mostly by themselves, but not totally. One day when

Thomas Merton was going into town for
something, he had a mystical experience
right there on the sidewalk. He wrote:
"At the corner of Fourth and Walnut, in
the center of the shopping district, I was
suddenly overwhelmed with the realization
that I loved all these people, that they were
mine and I theirs, that we could not be alien
to one another even though we were total
strangers."

People who have a mystical experience
don't always tell about it. Maybe they are
afraid they will be laughed at. No one
should laugh, even if they—the people
or their mystical experiences—seem not
exactly normal. It can be hard to find words
to explain a mystical experience.

C. My Experience
Sometimes we wonder about big
questions, the kind that can't be answered
during Question Time. What are we on
Earth for? Where did we come from?

215

Where do we go when we die? A mystical experience sometimes gives answers that are more like feelings than words. And this is what happened to me.

I had been trying to have a mystical experience for my report, but nothing was happening. I tried to see something different when I went for a walk with our dog, Cathode, but everything seemed ordinary. I tried to send a message across town with my brain, but it didn't work.

Then on Saturday my best friend and I had the scariest experience of our lives, and I am sure you all have probably heard what happened to us. This was very, very real. It was also, I think, the start of something unusual that happened to me on the next morning.

Sunday morning I woke up very early. I wasn't thinking about doing my report or about having a mystical experience at all. I was just too awake to go back to sleep, so I went outside. I started walking and ended up sitting on the top of Wolman Hill. From there I watched the sun rise, and I didn't think about anything else.

They say the sun rises so slowly that you can't see it move. I think this is only because everyone is in a hurry all the time. I tried very hard to be still, and twice I saw the sun move in the sky. I looked around me, and I remembered learning that the smallest stone is millions of years older than we are. I saw people getting up and starting their days, and it's like I saw them differently than I ever had before. I can't explain exactly what I felt, but everything I saw seemed tied to everything else, and everything was good, and everything made sense somehow.

A man called Meister Eckhart lived in Germany during the Middle Ages. Meister Eckhart saw what he called the oneness of everything, and that's kind of what I saw Sunday morning. Everything felt connected and extra alive.

One book explained that Meister

Eckhart's point could be summed up by saying that every bush is a burning bush and every tree is full of angels. I didn't see any burning bushes or angels Sunday morning, but I felt like everything was like the last line of the song "Joy to the World." The one that goes, "And heaven, and heaven, and nature sing."

D. What I Learned

The books I read at the library said most mystical experiences teach something. A person who has a real mystical experience is never the same afterwards. I would like to end my report with some things that I learned.

1) Parents are always saying "Be thankful," like for food and clothes and lots of stuff. It never means much until one day when you realize how important everything ordinary is. One day you wake up, like I did yesterday, and see how extraordinary the people that you see everyday are. How good it is just to be alive. Then you see that being thankful is very important, because ordinary things can be like miracles.

2) Everyone is a person just like you. That may seem obvious, but I mean they're like you even if they seem different or go to a different school or a different church or no church. Everyone matters and has feelings like you do. They might be lonely, or get tired, or just feel unconnected and need some attention sometimes.

3) It is bad to feel alone, but it is only a feeling. No one is an island. People are connected to everything there is—to the land, to the trees, the sky, and the stars— and to each other. Our school and our town is like a family, so is the world.

4) Maybe everyone can have a mystical experience, but a person shouldn't try to have a mystical experience. Trying won't make it happen. A friend of mine once said you can tell when you've had a real mystical experience because it will leave you better

than you were before. I think one way it will
leave you better is that you will think about
yourself less and think about other people
more.

———

After all the reports were finished, Mr. Phillips told us that we had all done a very good job. I wasn't sure, but it seemed like he had made a special look over at me when he said this.

Then Pastor Jill arrived. She was wearing pointed, green slippers, green tights, and a short, green elf's dress.

It's a fact: I understood why Mr. Phillips chose the name Babe for her.

She also had a red elf's hat on with a bell that jingled as she walked and a big plate of Christmas cookies with sprinkles. Mr. Phillips gave the class free time to talk and eat cookies until school was dismissed.

Just as the final bell rang, instead of saying, "Well, it's been real," Mr. Phillips and Pastor Jill stood together with their arms around each other's waist and said, "Well . . . have a real Merry Christmas!" And everyone laughed, including Mr. Phillips and Pastor Jill. Then they walked together to the back of the classroom and gave each student a hug or a handshake as we filed out towards the cloakroom.

———

We all put on our hats and coats, and everybody wished everybody else a Merry Christmas about a hundred times. As he was leaving to pick up Hannah Louise, Nitro told me that he felt good enough for some noodling and would come by my house later with his soccer ball. As he pointed out, it was never too early to start practicing for the game against Winston Elementary.

Finally I was heading down the hallway when I heard the sound of white Go-Goes on a pair of long legs running to catch up with me. I turned around.

"Hello, Leda . . . um, I mean, Jana."

"Oh, I'm not Jana anymore. I am back to being just Leda again."

"That's good," I said. "I mean, well, I mean I like you best as just Leda."

221

"Well, Todd Farrel, that is about the most cordial thing you have ever said to me." Leda paused for a moment and just smiled. Then she said, "I almost forgot. I've got something to give you."

Leda pulled an envelope from her backpack. "Here, open it," she said. "Mr. Phillips was totally serious when he told us that you didn't want anyone to make a big deal out of how you saved Nitro. But we wanted to give you a small token of our esteem anyway. I mean it's not as though something like this happens at St. Luke's every day. So, well, this is from all of us."

I took the envelope and opened it to find a handmade card inside. On the front of the card was a picture of two upside-down boots on top of a wavy line of water. The boots looked like the person wearing them had just dived under. I opened the card. On the left side were the words:

SUPERHERO #8: POLAR BOY
created by Davis Farrel

Superpower 1:
He can swim in freezing cold water.

Superpower 2:
If you need help, he is a good friend.

On the right side in big calligraphy letters were the words:

Very Nice Save, Todd! That Was Extraordinary!

Underneath everyone in the class had signed their name—including Mr. Phillips, Pastor Jill, and even the headmaster.

I got a little embarrassed, and I think I turned red, but I smiled as I read all the names. Leda had written hers really big. So had Nitro.

"The card is somewhat humorous, but we want you to know that we really mean it. Everyone is extremely proud of you, Todd," said Leda.

Then to my great surprise, Leda gave me a very small hug that lasted about one second.

Before you get any ideas, I should say that it was definitely not a romantic hug. But it was a hug all the same.

To my even greater surprise, I discovered that I

didn't mind it as much as I thought I would. Without getting all gushy, you could say I didn't mind it at all.

"Well, thanks, Leda," I said as I turned even more red. "Just tell everyone thanks a lot."

I found myself with nothing to say for a moment. To change the subject I asked, "So who were you, in your final identity?"

"I called my final identity Nada the Nothingness."

"What does Nada mean?"

"*Nada* is the Spanish word for nothing."

I thought for a moment. "So your name was really Nothing the Nothingness? Well, wouldn't that be kind of bad—I mean, being nothing?"

"Not necessarily. It can be kind of agreeable to just completely forget about yourself sometimes. It depends on your point of view."

I thought about this for a moment, then said, "I think I can see what you mean."

"You can?" asked Leda in surprise.

"Sure."

"You know, Todd, I really liked your report. It

was very acute."

"Thanks, Leda," I said, wondering exactly what acute meant—it sounded like something good. "I liked your report, too, 'Five Women Soccer Players of Renown.' Hey, my mom says it's okay to ask you to come over when your parents come for the Healthy Supper Club this Saturday night. Nitro is coming over with his parents."

"Gosh! I would really like that!" said Leda with a really big smile and a lot more excitement in her voice than I would have thought. Then we stood there together in the hallway and said nothing for a moment.

A moment that was, well, kind of shimmery.

Suddenly Leda looked up at the clock on the wall. "Yikes! I'm almost late, but first I have to tell you my good news. In the fall I tried out for Twenty-and-One, you know, the school hand bell choir, and I was chosen as our class's first alternate—which is good except, to be honest, all first alternate means is that you only get to play if someone drops out.

"Well, the good news is that Theresa Anwar's parents think she is doing too many things, and they

225

told her she had to either give up handbells or violin lessons. I suppose from her perspective that's bad news, but anyway, she decided to give up handbells, so Mrs. Jubal asked me Friday after school if I would like to play, and, well, look . . ."

Leda opened her backpack and pulled out a shiny brass bell.

"Usually they don't let you take them out of the chapel, where we practice, but I was so excited that I think she made an exception for me—since I am new to the group and all. Isn't it beautiful?" Leda put the bell into my hands.

"Each person gets to choose which one they want to play. Some people like the little, high-toned bells. Others want the bigger, low ones. The longer you are in the group the better selection you have, and some of the eighth graders play more than one bell.

"Because of my seniority, or actually my *juniority*, I had only one choice, but I don't care. It's Middle C, and I think that says something. Middle C is connected. Middle C is in the center. Middle C is part of the continent—you know, part of the main.

"Well, I have got to go." Leda stuffed the bell

back in her bag and zipped it up. "I don't want to be late for my first practice."

As Leda sprang off down the corridor, she yelled back over her shoulder, "Mrs. Jubal says it's never too early to start getting ready for our Valentine's Day concert! I'll see you Saturday!"

"See you Saturday," I called after her.

I started down the hall to the outside door once more. My head was a whirlwind of feelings about lots of things—not the least of which was my hug*ette* from Leda.

A moment later I heard the clear, sweet tone of Middle C ring out.

I looked behind to see Leda down at the end of the hallway holding up the shining bell. She gave me a wave then disappeared around the corner, the heels of her white boots kicking up behind her.

I waved back even though she was already gone.

Then turning, I pushed open the outside door. And I paused, and from somewhere, the words came to my mind: *A bell says to us, 'Pay attention— something special is happening.'*

Then with what Leda might have called the drollest smile on my face, I stepped through the doorway, out into the extraordinary, ordinary, bright, winter afternoon, out into the start of Christmas vacation.

To begin the long walk home.

Read More About It

Scholars have two theories about where the name Boxing Day came from.

Some say the term comes from the actual boxes that the gifts were put in, and this is how Mr. Phillips explains the name's origin. Pastor Jill refers to the other theory when she discusses the Poor Boxes from the back of churches which were opened on December 26th so that the money which had been collected inside could be distributed to the needy.

———

Geoffrey Chaucer lived in England during the 1300s

and has been called the father of English literature. When he died in the 1400, he left his most famous work, *The Canterbury Tales*, unfinished.

The story introduces twenty-four characters—the Oxford Cleric from Mr. Phillips' picture is one of them. All of them are setting out from London on a pilgrimage to Canterbury Cathedral to visit the tomb of St. Thomas a Beckett. To pass the time, each pilgrim was to tell two stories on the way to Canterbury and two on the way back.

———

John Donne lived in London two hundred years after Chaucer. His well known statement "No man is an island" is a part of a famous sermon titled Meditation 17. As Mrs. Whitmore would have pointed out, Donne certainly meant no man or woman or boy or girl is an island. But it's not quite as memorable this way. Here is the passage the sentence comes from:

No man is an island entire of itself;
every man is a piece of the continent, a part
of the main. If a clod be washed away by

the sea, Europe is the less as well as if a
promontory were, as well as if a manor of
thy friend's or of thine own were. Any man's
death diminishes me, because I am involved
in mankind. And therefore never send to
know for whom the bell tolls; it tolls for
thee.

———

Carl Jung was a Swiss psychiatrist who lived from 1875 to 1961. He included a large role for the mystical in his treatment of patients. The rock star Sting and his band The Police recorded a song called "Synchronicity" that featured Jung's concept.

Dr. Jung had a famous plaque in his office which later served as the epitaph on his gravestone. In Latin it said *Vocatus atque non vocatus Deus aderit*. This can be translated as: Invited or not, God is present.

———

Thomas Merton was an English teacher at a Catholic boys school, but when he was 26, he became a monk at the Abbey of Our Lady of Gethsemane near Bardstown, Kentucky. The story of his spiritual journey became a best-selling book called *The Seven Story Mountain*. The epiphany which he had is described in Todd's report. The quote Todd used comes from Merton's book *Conjectures of a Guilty Bystander*.

———

Robert Hayden, the Revolutionary Was soldier whose gravestone was used for the rubbing, is a fictional character. But the writing on the tombstone comes from the last words of Robert Emmett, an Irish hero who fought against the English. You can see Robert Emmett's speech on the eve of his execution at www.robertemmet.org/speech.htm.

———

Good King Wenceslas (907-935) was actually the Duke of Bohemia. He was a strongly moral man who believed that his faith needed to be put into action in practical ways. After being murdered in front of the door to the cathedral in Prague, he became Bohemia's most famous martyr and patron saint.

The song the Concert Choir sings describes King

Wenceslas braving a fierce storm to help a poor neighbor. It ends with the message that when we seek to help those less fortunate, we shall ourselves find a blessing. Should you ever visit Prague, which is the capital of the Czech Republic, you can see where he is buried inside St. Vitus Cathedral.

———

The passage that Leda used with her rubbing, "Macavity's the Mystery Cat," comes from *Old Possum's Book of Practical Cats* by T. S. Eliot. This book was the basis for the Broadway musical *Cats*, which Leda certainly would have gone with her parents to see.

———

Many people think Pele was the greatest soccer player that ever lived. He was born in Brazil in 1940, and his family was very poor. As a boy when he wasn't practicing soccer, he would shine shoes for pennies. Pele went on to break almost every record in professional soccer. He was known for his excellent dribbling and his amazing head shots.

The idea for Nitro's Famous Backwards Reverse

Pass comes from a famous poster of Pele making a pass much like the one that Nitro finally makes.

———

Mia Hamm is the highest scoring women's soccer player in the world and is considered one of greatest female athletes of all time. When she was 15, she became the youngest woman in history to play on the U.S. national team. She is best known for leading the U.S. women's team to the gold medal in the 1996 Olympics.